20th Century-Fox
Presents

A MAX L. RAAB—SI LITVINOFF PRODUCTION

WALKABOUT

Starring
JENNY AGUTTER
LUCIEN JOHN
DAVID GUMPILIL

Executive Producer
MAX L. RAAB

Produced By
SI LITVINOFF

Directed & Photographed By
NICHOLAS ROEG

Screenplay By
EDWARD BOND

Based on the Novel By
JAMES VANCE MARSHALL

Music By
JOHN BARRY

COLOR BY DE LUXE®

A MAX L. RAAB-SI LITVINOFF PRODUCTION

WALKABOUT

**An unforgettable novel
by James Vance Marshall,
now a motion picture by
Twentieth-Century Fox.**

". . . Succeeds very well in arousing our sympathy
and understanding."

—Elizabeth Janeway

"Besides using *Walkabout* to point a sound moral,
Mr. Marshall makes it the vehicle for some fasci-
nating glimpses of the wildlife of a region he must
know intimately and love deeply."

—Dan Wickenden

"Written in an effectively simple style, showing
keen psychological insight, interesting glimpses of
aboriginal customs, and vivid pictures of the flora,
fauna and terrain of the Australian bush . . ."

—*Booklist*

By the same author

A RIVER RAN OUT OF EDEN
MY BOY JOHN THAT WENT TO SEA
A WALK TO THE HILLS OF
    THE DREAMTIME

WALKABOUT

by
James Vance Marshall

Belmont Books   •   New York City

WALKABOUT
A BELMONT BOOK—JUNE, 1971

Published by

Belmont Productions, Inc.
185 Madison Avenue
New York, New York 10016

Library of Congress Catalog Card Number 72-131932

Printed in the United States of America.

Published by special arrangement
with William Morrow and Company, Inc.

CHAPTER ONE

It was silent and dark, and the children were afraid.

They huddled together, their backs to an outcrop of rock. Far below them, in the bed of the gully, a little stream flowed inland—soon to peter out in the vastness of the Australian desert. Above them the walls of the gully climbed smooth to a moonless sky.

The little boy nestled more closely against his sister. He was trembling.

She felt for his hand and gave it a reassuring squeeze. "All right, Peter," she whispered. "I'm here."

She felt the tension ebb slowly out of him, the trembling die gradually away. When a boy is only eight a big sister of thirteen can be wonderfully comforting.

"Mary," he whispered, "I'm hungry. Let's have something to eat."

The girl sighed. She felt in the pocket of her dress and pulled out a paper-covered piece of stick candy. It was their last one. She broke it, gave him half, and slipped the other half back in her pocket.

"Don't bite," she whispered. "Suck."

Why they were whispering they didn't know. Perhaps because everything was so very silent, like a church. Or was it because they were afraid: afraid of being heard?

For a while the only sounds were the distant rippling of water over stone and the sucking of lips around a diminishing stick of candy. Then the boy started to fidget, moving restlessly from foot to foot. Again the girl reached for his hand.

"Aren't you comfortable, Pete?"

"No."

"What is it?"

"My leg's bleeding again. I can feel the wet."

She bent down. The handkerchief she had tied around his thigh was now draped like a recalcitrant garter over his ankle. She refastened it, and they huddled together, holding hands, looking into the powdery blackness of the Australian night.

They could see nothing. They could hear nothing—apart from the lilt of the rivulet—for it was still too early for the stirring of bush life. Later there'd be other sounds: the hoot of the mopoke, the mating howl of the dingo, and the leathery flip-flap-flip of the wings of flying foxes. But now, an hour after sunset, the bush was silent, frighteningly still: full, to the children, of terrors all the greater for being unknown. It was a far cry from here to their comfortable home in South Carolina in the suburbs of Charleston.

Time passed slowly, until at last the boy's head dropped to his sister's lap. He snuggled closer. His breathing became slower and deeper. Eventually he slept.

The girl, however, refused to let herself sleep; that would never have done, for she had to stand guard. She was the elder. The responsibility was hers. That was the way it had always been, as far back as she could remember. Always she had been the big sister who had stuck plaster on Peter's knees, had taught him to tie his shoelaces, and had taken the lead in their games of Indians and cowboys. Now that they were lost—somewhere in the middle of an unknown continent—the weight of her responsibility was greater than ever. A wave of tenderness welled up inside her. Always she had big-sistered him; now she would have to mother him as well.

She sat staring into the darkness that was warm, thick and almost tangible, until at last her mind became utterly blank. The day's events had been too overwhelming, had drawn on her too heavily. The rhythmic beat of the small boy's slumber came to her lullingly now. Gradually her breathing fell into step with his. The whisper of the creek came to her like the croon of a lullaby. Her eyelids drooped and closed, fluttered and closed again. Soon she too was asleep.

In the darkness beyond the gully, the bush came slowly to life.

A lumbering wombat came creeping out of his ground den. His short stumpy body forced a way through the underscrub, his long food-foraging snout plowing through the sandy earth in search of his favorite roots. Suddenly he stopped, sniffed; his nostrils dilated. He followed the strange new scent. Soon he came to the gully. He looked the children over, thoughtfully, not hungrily, for he was a vegetarian, an eater of roots. His curiosity satisfied, he shambled away.

Random fireflies zigzagged by, their night-lights flickering like sparklets from a roving toy-sized forge.

Soon, creeping along the edge of darkness, came another creature, a marsupial tiger cat, her eyes widened by the night to oriflammes of fire. She too had scented the children; she too clambered into the gully and looked them over. They smelled young and tender and tempting, but they were large; too bulky, she decided, to drag back to her mewling litter. Disappointed, she slunk away.

A night mist tried to gather, failed—for the air in the gully was too warm—and dissipated into pre-dawn dew. The dampness settled on the children, pressing down their clothes, tracing the outline of their bodies in tiny globules of pearl. They stirred but didn't wake. They were lost in their dreams.

In her sleep the girl moved uneasily. She was in the airplane again, and she knew that something was wrong. She and Peter were the only passengers, sandwiched between the crates of vegetables and the frozen carcasses of beef, and she was watching the port engine, waiting for the flames she knew would come. Too soon they were there, the tiny tongues of red licking out of the cowling. In her sleep she twisted and moaned; then mercifully her mind went blank—nature's safety valve that protects, even in dreams, those who have been shocked beyond endurance—and the next thing she dreamed was that she and Peter were staggering away from the blazing plane, she pulling him frantically because one of his legs was numb and his feet kept sinking into the soft red sand. "Quick, Peter," she gasped. "Quick, before it explodes." She heard a dull pulsating roar and, looking back, saw the figure of the navigating officer carrying the pilot and clambering out of the wreckage. In the heat of the explosion he glowed white-hot, disintegrating. Again her mind went numb, but in her sleep she clutched her brother's hand; clutched it and squeezed it so tight that he half-woke and slid awkwardly off her lap.

The night-lights of the fireflies grew pale and anemic. Out of the east crept a permeating mother-of-pearl: the sunup of another day.

CHAPTER TWO

The advance guard of sunlight filtered into the gully, turning the night to powdery opaqueness. The warmth of the rays drew this opaqueness up into little spirals of mist—random smoke rings from a giant's pipe, that floated lazily over the billabong.

As the light gained in intensity, the bush beyond the gully took on new colors; vivid colors: jade and emerald, white and green, crimson, scarlet and gold. Here was something very different from the desert of popular imagination; a flowering wilderness of eucalyptus, lantana, brigalow and ironbark. First to take color were the tops of the eucalyptus: great two-hundred-foot relics of the forests of antiquity, their trunks skeleton white, their oil-laden leaves already twisting edge-on to dodge the shriveling rays of the sun. The light moved lower, gilding the flowered lantana and the straggling brigalow as they intertwined in age-old rivalry; then it came lower still, warming the ridged and furrowed ironbark, the tree that is hard as studded rhinoceros hide, the tree that never dies (so the Aboriginals say) and is scented more sweetly than orange blossom. At last the golden rays flooded past the outcrop of rock and over the still sleeping children.

The girl lay leaning against the rock. But the boy had

moved in the night; he lay sprawled on his back now, arms and legs akimbo. Both slept soundly, unconscious of the growing beauty of the Australian dawn.

On the topmost branch of a gum tree that overhung the gully, there alighted a bird: a large, gray-backed bird, with tufted poll and outsized beak. Its eyes, swiveling separately, searched the gully for food; but instead of the hoped-for frog or snake sunning itself on the rock, it saw the children. The kookaburra was puzzled. The presence of these strange interlopers, it decided, deserved to be announced. It opened wide its beak, and a continuous flow of grating, unmelodious notes shattered the calm of the gully.

The girl leaped to her feet. Her heart pounded. The sweat broke out on the palms of her hands. Terrified, she stared round the sunlit gully.

High above, the kookaburra noted her reactions. Its curiosity was piqued. With another ear-splitting shriek it came swooping down.

The girl relaxed. It was only a bird. Its scream was nothing to be frightened of; more to be laughed at really.

She turned to Peter. The kookaburra hadn't disturbed his sleep. Lying beneath the great slab of rock, he looked small and helpless, dwarfed by the immensity of his surroundings. Once again pity and tenderness welled up inside her; brought a pricking feeling to the back of her eyes. How utterly he depended on her now. When he wakes, she thought, he'll be hungry; as hungry as I am. Feeling in the pocket of her frock, she took out the last half-stick of candy; gently she slipped it into her brother's pocket.

Food, she realized, was their immediate problem.

Water they could get from the billabong, but what could they eat? She knew that people who didn't eat, died. She'd read about an explorer once . . . it didn't take many days. She looked at the kookaburra. As if sensing her thoughts, he gave a piercing shriek and went winging down the gully.

But other birds soon took his place: big, black-bodied cockatoos with yellow tails, ripping bark off the eucalyptus in search of grubs; gang-gangs dangling upside down from the flowers of the lantana; and iridescent painted finches, splashing merrily in the shallow waters of the stream. The girl watched them. She envied the finches. Already the sun was warm; her dress was dirty and clammy with dew; and the water looked cool and crystal-clear: cool, crystal-clear and tempting. She looked carefully around. Peter was asleep; there was probably no one else within a hundred miles. Impulsively she kicked off her sandals, pulled her dress over her head, stepped out of her pants and ran naked down to the water. The finches darted away. She had the creek to herself.

She found a shallow pool, immediately below a miniature waterfall. Here she slid into the water, watching the ripples lap slowly higher over her knees, thighs and waist. She was breast-deep before her toes touched bottom. Looking down she could see her underwater-self with startling clarity, could even see the bruise on her hip—where she'd crashed against the side of the plane—standing out darkly against the white of her skin. She ducked down till only her floating hair showed on the surface, her long golden hair, the color of ripening corn, which she started to swirl around and about her like the mulcta of a matador. She laughed and splashed and hand-scooped the water over her face and forgot she was hungry.

Beside the outcrop of rock, her brother stirred. Half-asleep, half-awake, he heard the splash of water. He sat up, yawning and rubbing the sleepiness out of his eyes. For a moment he couldn't think where he was. Then he caught sight of his sister.

"Look out, Mary!" he yelled. "I'm coming too."

He scrambled up. Sandals, shorts and shirt were flung aside as he came charging down to the stream. With a reckless belly flop he arrived beside the girl in a shower of drenching spray.

Mary wasn't pleased. Seizing him under the armpits, she plonked him back on the bank.

"Peter, you shouldn't. It's too deep. Look, you're full of water."

"I'm not. I spit it out. Besides, I can swim."

He belly flopped a second time into the pool. But Mary noticed he kept to the shallows now: to the sandy-bottomed shallows where the rivulet widened and the banks flattened out. Watching him, she suddenly became conscious of her nakedness. Quickly she scrambled out of the pool and struggled into her dress.

Peter surveyed her critically.

"You're all wet," he said. "You ought to have dried yourself first."

"Stop jabbering. And get dry yourself."

She helped him out of the pool and rubbed him down with his shirt.

"I'm hungry," he announced cheerfully. "What can we eat?"

"There's candy in your pocket."

He pulled out the sticky fragment.

"It's not much."

He broke it and dutifully offered her half. But she shook her head.

"It's all right," she said. "I've had mine."

She watched him as, cheeks bulging, hands in pockets, he went strolling down the creek. Thank heavens he didn't seem to be worried: not yet. Whatever happened he must never realize how worried she was; must never lose faith in her ability to look after him.

She watched him exploring their strange surroundings; watched him drop flat on his stomach, and knew he was Davy Crockett, reconnoitering a new frontier. He wiggled along in the sand, cautiously peering across to the farther bank of the stream. Suddenly he leaped to his feet, clutched the seat of his trousers and gave a yell of anguish. Again and again he yelled, as again and again red-hot needles of pain shot through his squirming body.

Mary tumbled and slithered down the rock to his aid. For a second she couldn't think what had happened; then she too felt the red-hot needle of pain, and looking down saw their assailants. Ants. Jumping ants. Three quarters of an inch long, 40 percent jaw and 40 percent powerful grass-hopperish legs. She saw their method of attack at once, saw how they hunched themselves up, then catapulted through the air—often several feet—onto their prey. She half-dragged, half-carried Peter away, at the same time hauling off his trousers.

"It's all right," she gasped. "They're only ants. Look. Hanging on to your trousers. Biting away as if you're still inside."

His wailing stopped; he looked at his discarded shorts. It was true. The ants were still there; their wispy antennaes weaving from side to side like the arms of so many punch-drunk boxers; their mandibles were open wide, eager to bite again. But they weren't given the chance. With a shout of rage Peter elbowed his sister aside and started to jump on the shorts; his feet thudded into the denim, pounding and crushing, pulverizing the ants to death. Or so he thought.

Mary stood aside; relieved, half-amused at the violence of his revenge. She had seen the ants sneaking clear of the shorts, but she said nothing. Not until his pounding feet threatened to damage his trousers. Then she reached for his hand.

"Okay, Peter. They're all dead now."

She helped him on with his shorts.

He started to whimper then; the pain of the bites touching off a host of half-formed fears. Mary's arms went round him. He felt small and shivery and thin; she could feel his heart thudding between his ribs.

"It's all right," she whispered. "I won't let them bite you again."

His sobs died; but only momentarily. Then they restarted.

"What is it, Pete?"

"I don't like this place."

Now it's coming, she thought. It's coming, and there's nothing I can do about it.

"I don't like it here, Mary. I want to go home."

"But we can't go home, Peter. We've nothing to cross the sea in."

"Then let's go to Uncle Keith. In Adelaide."

She was surprised how much he'd remembered. Their

plar

K

? N

"Yes," she said, "nov

laide."

CHAPTER THREE

Sturt Plain, where the airplane had crashed, is in the center of the Northern Territory. It is roughly twice the size of Texas; but instead of some 10,000,000 inhabitants, it has less than 35,000, and instead of some thousands of roads, it has two, of which one is a fair-weather stock route. Most of the inhabitants are grouped around three small towns—Tennant Creek, Hooker Creek and Daly Waters; which means that the rest of the area is virtually uninhabited. The Plain is 1400 miles from Adelaide and not a good place to be lost in.

Had they known enough to weigh up their chances, the children would have realized their only hope was to stay beside the wrecked plane; to rely on rescue from the air. But this never occurred to them. Adelaide was somewhere to the south. So southward they started to walk.

The girl worked things out quietly and sensibly—she wasn't the sort to get in a panic. The sun had risen there, on the left of the gully, so that would be east. South, then, must be straight ahead; downstream. That was lucky. Perhaps they'd be able to follow the creek all the way to the sea, all the way to Adelaide. She knotted the four corners of Peter's handkerchief, dipped it in the water and draped it over his head—for already the sun was uncomfortably hot.

"Come on, Peter," she said, "let's go."

She led the way down the gully.

At first the going was easy. Close to the stream, rocks of granite and quartz provided safe footing, and the trees, sprouting from every pocket of clay, were thick enough to give a welcome shade, but not so thick that they hindered progress. Mary pushed steadily on.

Soon the gully became wider, flatter, fanning into an open plain. Another rivulet, full after the recent forty-eight hours of annual rain, joined theirs, and together the two of them went looping away down a shallow, sand-fringed valley. In the middle of the valley the undergrowth was thick. Briars and underbrush slowed down their progress. But Mary didn't want to lose sight of the stream. Determinedly she forced a way through the tangle of vegetation, turning every now and then to give her brother a hand. Ground vines coiled and snaked and clutched at their feet; the decaying trunks of fallen trees perversely blocked their path; but the girl kept on, following the line of least resistance, holding back the lower branches to protect Peter from their swing back.

For two hours the boy followed her manfully; then he started to lag. Mary noticed at once; she cut across to the stream and sat down on a shelving slab of quartz.

"We'll rest now," she said.

Thankfully he collapsed beside her. She smoothed the hair out of his eyes, plastering it back with its own sweat.

For a long time there was silence; then came the question she had been dreading.

"I'm hungry. Mary. What we going to eat?"

"Oh, Peter! It's not lunchtime yet."

"When will it be?"

"I'll tell you when."

But he wasn't satisfied; not satisfied at all.

"When it is time, what we going to eat?"

"I'll find something."

She didn't tell him that ever since leaving the gully she'd been searching for berries, in vain. But he sensed her anxiety. His mouth started to droop.

"I'm hungry now," he said.

Quickly she got up.

"All right. Let's look for something to eat."

To start with—at least for the boy—it was an amusing game: part of their Big Adventure. They looked in the stream for fish; but the fish, such as they were, were asleep: invisible in the sediment-mud. They looked in the bush for animals, but the animals were all asleep, avoiding the heat of the sun in carefully chosen burrow, log or cave. They looked among the riverside rocks for lizards, but the reptiles heard their clumsy approach and slid soundlessly into crack or crevice. The bush slept: motionless, silent, apparently deserted, drugged to immobility by the heat of the midday sun.

The game wasn't amusing for very long.

Eventually their search led them away from the stream, into less luxuriant vegetation in the open bush. They could see farther here; could see to where, a little way ahead, a ridge of low, slab-sided hills were tilted out of the level plain. The children stared at the hills. They looked friendly; familiar; like the mountains of Maine, which they often visited during summer vacation. The boy reached for his sister's hand.

"Mary!"

"What is it, Pete?"

"Remember when Daddy took us to Maine?

Remember all the ocean we could see from the top of that great big hill?''

"I remember."

"Maybe we could see the ocean from the tops of those mountains."

It took them half an hour to get to the foot of the hills. They rose in a low escarpment, an outcrop of granite and quartz, jutting abruptly out of the level plain. The stream, moat-like, skirted their feet. There seemed at first to be no way up. Then the girl spotted a dark shadow: a gully, cleaving the escarpment like the cut of an axe.

Except that it faced north rather than south, it might have been the gully where they had spent the night; it had the same smoothly rising sides, and the same rock-fringed tumbling stream. It took them four hours to climb it.

If the stream hadn't provided them with water, and the sides of the gully with shade, they would never have got to the top.

As it was, the sun was setting as they clambered on to the rim of the hills and saw the country to southward stretching away in front of them, bathed in golden light: a magnificent panorama, a scene of primeval desolation, mile after hundred mile of desert, sand and scrub. And in the far distance, pools of silver; pools of glinting, shimmering light, pools which shivered, wavered and contracted, and seemed to hang a fraction above the horizon.

The boy danced with delight.

"Look, Mary. Look! The ocean. The ocean. It isn't far to go."

She caught hold of him and pulled him against her and

pressed his face to her breasts.

"Don't look, Peter," she whispered. "Don't look again. It isn't fair."

She knew what the pools of silver were: the salt pans of the great Australian desert. She sat down on the thin tufted grass and started to roll and unroll the hem of her frock.

After a long time she got up and led the protesting Peter back to the gully. At least there was water there. Tomorrow, she told him, they would walk on down to the ocean. Tomorrow they wouldn't be hungry anymore.

CHAPTER FOUR

Sunup brought the kookaburras, the gang-gangs and the finches. It brought warmth and color. And hunger.

The girl woke early. She lay on her back, thinking. Outwardly she was calm, but inwardly she was damming back a gathering flood of fear. Always she had protected Peter, had smoothed things out and made them easy for him—mollycoddled him like an anxious hen, her father had once said. But how could she protect him now? She knew that soon he'd be awake; awake and demanding they start off for the "ocean." It would be too cruel to tell him the ocean wasn't there. She'd have to think of something else, have to tell him one of those special sort of lies that Mommy said God didn't mind. Her forehead puckered in thought.

Too soon Peter was awake.

They spent the morning foraging for food. It would be foolish, Mary said, to start walking without having something to eat; without first collecting a stock of food for their journey. The ocean might be farther off than it looked.

They searched mainly for fruit, but for a long time found nothing. They examined the tawny leopard trees, the sapless mellowbane, the humble bushes with their frightened collapsing leaves, and the bloodwoods with their overflowing crimson sap. They skirted the kurrajongs and the bottlebrushes and the eucalyptus; then they came to a group of trees of another, rarer kind: graceful, symmetrical trees, covered with thick silver foliage and—miracle of miracles—with multicolored globules of fruit.

Peter gave a whoop of delight and rushed headlong at the longed-for food. For a second Mary hung back, thinking of poison, then she too was leaping and snatching at the balls of fruit. It was a chance they'd have to take.

The fruit—called *quondong* by the Aboriginals—was about the size of Ping-Pong balls and ranged in color from greengage green to plum red. The redder fruit, they quickly found, were the riper. To the starving children they were ambrosia; sweet and juicy, thirst-quenching and nourishing. They ate, and ate, and ate.

For a long time they sat in the shade of the *quondong* trees, the trees that had saved their lives. They were too happy to talk.

After a while Mary got up and began to pick more of the fruit—their cache for the trek to the ocean. She hummed contentedly as she collected the *quondong*, storing them first in Peter's handkerchief then in the folds of her dress. Soon Peter also got up; he wandered across to one of the trees and started lazily to gather the fruit. Working their way from tree to tree, the children drifted slowly apart.

Though the edge had gone from his hunger, Peter wasn't altogether at ease. He kept looking nervously at the surrounding bush. He had a strange sort of feeling, a feeling of being watched. Several times he looked up quickly, certain there was someone there, but the bush slept on in the heat of the sun: silent, motionless, apparently deserted. Unconvinced, he sidled back to his sister.

"Mary!" he whispered. "I think there's somebody here!"

"Somebody here! Where?"

Disbelieving she swung round. The *quondong* fell to the grass. Only by snapping her teeth together did she stifle a scream of fear. For there, less than four feet away, so close that she could have stretched out an arm and touched him, was a boy. Ebony black and naked.

CHAPTER FIVE

The girl's first impulse was to grab Peter and run, but as her eyes swept over the stranger, her fear died away. The boy was young—certainly no older than she was; he was unarmed, and his attitude was more inquisitive than threatening, more puzzled than hostile.

He wasn't the least bit like the Negroes back home. His skin was certainly black, but beneath it was a curious hint of undersurface bronze, and it was fine-grained, glossy, satiny, almost silklike. His hair wasn't crinkly but nearly straight, and his eyes were blue-black: big, soft and inquiring. In his hand was a baby rock wallaby, its eyes, unclosed in death, staring vacantly above a tiny pointed snout.

All this Mary noted and accepted. The thing that she couldn't accept, the thing that seemed to her shocking and altogether wrong, was the fact that the boy was naked.

The three children stood looking at one another in the middle of the Australian desert. Motionless as the outcrops of granite they stared, and stared, and stared. Between them the distance was less than the spread of an outstretched arm, but more than 100,000 years.

Brother and sister were products of the highest stratum of mankind's evolution. In them the primitive had long ago been swept aside, been submerged by mechanization, swamped by scientific development, nullified by the standardized pattern of the white man's way of life. They had climbed a long way up the ladder of progress; they had climbed so far, in fact, that they had forgotten how their climb had started. Coddled in babyhood, psychoanalyzed in childhood, nourished on predigested patent foods, provided with continuous push-button entertainment, the basic realities of life were something they'd never had to face.

It was very different with the Aboriginal. He knew what reality was. He led a way of life that was already old when Tut-ankh-amen was laid in his pyramid, a way of life that had been tried and proved before the white man's continents were lifted out of the sea. Among the secret water holes of the Australian desert his people had lived and died, unchanged and unchanging, for 20,000 years. Their lives were unbelievably simple. They had no homes, no crops, no clothes, no possessions. The few things they had, they shared: food and wives, children and laughter, tears and hunger and thirst. They walked from one water hole to the next; they exhausted one supply of food, then moved on to another. Their lives were utterly uncomplicated because they were devoted to one purpose, dedicated in their entirety to the waging of one battle—the battle with death. Death was their ever-present enemy. He sought them out from every dried-up salt pan, from the flames of every bush fire. He was never far away. Keeping him at bay was the Aboriginals' full-time job; the job they'd been doing for twenty thousand years; the job they were good at.

The desert sun streamed down. The children stared and stared.

Mary had decided not to move. To move would be a sign of weakness. She remembered being told about the man who had come face to face with a lion and had stared it out until it had slunk discomfited away. That was what she'd do to the black boy; she'd stare at him until he felt the shame of his nakedness and slunk away. She thrust out her chin and glared.

Peter had decided to take his cue from his sister. Clutching her hand he stood waiting—waiting for something to happen.

The Aboriginal was in no hurry. Time had little value to him. His next meal—the rock wallaby—was assured. Water was near. Tomorrow was also a day. For the moment he was content to examine these strange creatures at his leisure. Their clumsy, lumbering movements intrigued him; their lack of weapons indicated their harmlessness. His eyes moved slowly, methodically from one to another, examining them from head to foot. They were the first white people a member of his tribe had ever seen.

Mary, beginning to resent this scrutiny, intensified her glare. But the bush boy seemed in no way perturbed; his appraisal went methodically on.

After a while Peter started to fidget. The delay was fraying his nerves. He wished someone would do something, wished something would happen. Then, quite involuntarily, he himself started a new train of events. His head began to waggle, his nose tilted skyward; he spluttered and choked; he tried to hold his breath, but all in vain. It had to come. He sneezed.

It was a mighty sneeze for such a little boy, all the more violent for having been so long dammed back.

To his sister the sneeze was a calamity. She had just

intensified her stare to the point—she felt sure—of irresistibility, when the spell was shattered. The bush boy's attention shifted from her to Peter.

Frustration warped her sense of justice. She condemned her brother out of court, was turning on him angrily, when a second sneeze, even mightier than the first, shattered the silence of the bush.

Mary raised her eyes to heaven, invoking the gods as witnesses to her despair. But the vehemence of the second sneeze was still tumbling leaves from the humble bushes, when a new sound made her whirl around—a gust of laughter, melodious laughter; low at first, then becoming louder, unrestrained, disproportionate, uncontrolled.

She looked at the bush boy in amazement. He was doubled up with belly-shaking spasms of mirth.

Peter's incongruous, out-of-proportion sneeze had touched off one of his peoples' most highly developed traits: a sense of the ridiculous, a sense so keenly felt as to be almost beyond control. The bush boy laughed with complete abandon. He flung himself to the ground. He rolled head-over-heels in unrestrained delight.

His mirth was infectious. It woke in Peter an instant response: a like appreciation of the ludicrous. The guilt that the little boy had started to feel melted away. At first apologetically, then wholeheartedly, he too started to laugh.

The barrier of 20,000 years vanished in the twinkling of an eye.

The boys' laughter echoed back from the granite rocks. They started to strike comic postures, each striving to outdo the other in grotesque abandon.

Mary watched them. She would have dearly loved to

join in. A year ago—in her tomboy days—she would have. But not now. She was too sensible, too grown-up. Yet not grown-up enough to be free of an instinctive longing to share in the fun, to throw convention to the winds and join the capering jamboree. This longing she repressed. She stood aloof, waiting for them to stop. At last she went up to Peter and took his hand.

"That's enough, Peter," she said.

The skylarking subsided. For a moment there was silence, then the bush boy spoke.

"Worumgala?" (Where do you come from?) His voice was lilting as his laughter.

Mary and Peter looked at each other blankly.

The bush boy tried again.

"Worum mwa?" (Where are you going?)

It was Peter, not Mary, who floundered into the field of conversation.

"We don't know what you're saying. But we're lost. We want to go to Adelaide. That's where Uncle Keith lives. Which way do we go?"

The black boy grinned. To him the little one's voice was as comic as his appearance: half-gabble, half-chirp, and shrill, like a baby magpie's. Peter grinned back, eager for another orgy of laughter. But the bush boy wanted to be serious now. He stepped noiselessly up to Peter, brushed his fingers over the boy's face, then looked at them expectantly; but to his surprise the whiteness hadn't come off. He ran his fingers through Peter's hair. Again he was surprised—neither powdered clay, nor red-ochre paste. He turned his attention to the white boy's clothes.

Peter was by no means perturbed. On the contrary, he felt flattered, almost proud. He realized that the bush boy had never seen anything like him before. He held himself very straight, swelled out his chest and turned slowly around and around.

The bush boy's tapering fingers plucked gently at his shirt, following the line of the seams, testing the strength of the crisscross weave, exploring the mystery of the buttonholes. Then his attention passed from shirt to shorts. Peter became suddenly loquacious.

"Those are shorts. You ought to have 'em too. Aren't there any stores around here?"

The bush boy refused to be diverted. He had found the broad band of elastic that kept the shorts in place. While he fingered it, the white boy prattled on.

"That's elastic, keeps the shorts in place. It stretches. Look!"

He stuck his thumbs into the waistband, pulled the elastic away from his hips, then let it fly back. The resounding smack made the bush boy jump. Thoroughly pleased with himself Peter repeated the performance, this time adding a touch of pantomime, staggering backward as if he'd been struck. The black boy saw the joke. He grinned, but this time he kept his laughter under control, for his examination was a serious business. He ended up with a detailed inspection of Peter's sandals.

Then he turned to Mary.

It was the moment the girl had been dreading.

Yet she didn't draw back. She wanted to; God alone knew how she wanted to. Her nerves were strung taut. The idea of being manhandled by a naked black boy appalled her, struck at the root of one of the basic principles of her so-called civilized code. It was terrifying, revolting, obscene. Back home it could have got the black boy lynched. Yet she didn't move; not even when the dark fingers ran like spiders up and down her body.

She stayed motionless because, deep-down, she knew she had nothing to fear. For the warnings which had been drummed into her back home were somehow not applicable in the desert, and the values she had been taught to cherish had become suddenly meaningless. A little guilty, a little resentful, and more than a little bewildered, she waited passively for whatever might happen next.

The bush boy's inspection didn't take long. The larger of these strange creatures, he saw at once, was much the same as the smaller—except that the queer things draped around it were, if possible, even more ludicrous. Almost perfunctorily his fingers ran over Mary's face, frock and sandals, then he stepped back: satisfied. There was nothing more he wanted to know.

Turning to where the dead rock wallaby lay in the sand, he picked it up. Odd ants had found it and were nosing through its fur. The boy brushed them off. Then he walked quietly away, away down the valley. Soon he was out of sight.

The children couldn't believe it, couldn't believe that he'd really left them. It was so sudden, so utterly unexpected.

Peter was first to grasp what had happened.

"Mary!" His voice was frightened. "He's gone!"

The girl said nothing. She was torn by conflicting emotions. Relief that the naked black boy had disappeared, and regret that she hadn't asked him for help; fear that nobody could help them anyhow, and a sneaking feeling that perhaps if anyone could, it had been the black boy. A couple of days ago she'd have known what to do; known what was best and how to act. But she didn't know now. Uncertain, she hid her face in her hands.

It was Peter who made the decision. In the bush boy's laughter he'd found something he liked: a lifeline he didn't intend to lose.

"Come on, Mary!" he gasped. "Let's go after him!"

He went crashing into the bush. Slowly, doubtfully, his sister followed.

"Hey there!" Peter's reedy treble echoed down the valley. "We want to come too. Wait for us!"

"Hey, there!" the rocks reechoed. "Wait for us. Wait for us. Wait for us."

CHAPTER SIX

The bush boy turned. He knew what the call meant; the strangers were coming after him, were following him down the valley. Already he could hear them crashing and lumbering through the scrub.

He waited, relaxed both physically and mentally, one hand passed behind his back and closed around the opposite elbow; one foot, ostrich-like, resting on the calf of the opposite leg. He wasn't frightened, for he knew instinctively that the strangers were harmless as a pair of tailless kangaroos; but he *was* mildly surprised, for he had thought them both, especially the larger, eager to be on their way. As the children came racing toward him, he dropped his foot to the ground, became suddenly all attention, full of curiosity to know what they wanted to say and how they were going to say it.

Peter launched into a breathless appeal.

"Don't leave us, please! We're lost. We want food, an' water. And we want to know how to get to Adelaide."

Mary looked at the bush boy, and saw in his eyes a gleam of amusement. It angered her, for she knew the cause: Peter's high-pitched, Southern voice. All the tenets of progressive society and racial superiority combined inside her to form a deep-rooted core of resentment. It was wrong, cruelly wrong, that she and

51

her brother should be forced to run for help to a naked Negro. She clutched Peter's hand, half-drawing him away.

But Peter was obsessed by none of his sister's scruples. To him their problem was simple, uncomplicated: they wanted help, and here was someone who could, his instinct told him, provide it. The fact that his appeal had failed to register the first time nonplused him for a moment. But he wasn't put off; he stuck to his guns. Breath and composure regained, he now spoke slowly, in a lower, less excited key.

"Look, we're lost. We want water. You know water? War-tur. War-tur."

He cupped his hands together, drew them up to his lips, and went through the motions of swallowing.

The bush boy nodded.

"*Arkooloola.*"

His eyes were serious now: understanding and sympathetic. He knew what it meant to be thirsty.

"*Arkooloola.*"

He said the word again. Softly, musically, like the rippling of water over rock. He pursed up his lips and moved them as though he, too, were drinking.

Peter hopped delightedly from foot to foot.

"You've got it. *Arkooloolya.* That's what we want. And food too. You know food? Foo-ood. Foo-ood."

He went through the motions of cutting with knife and fork, then started to champ his jaws.

The cutting meant nothing to the bush boy; but the jaw champing did. Again his eyes were sympathetic.

"*Yeemara.*"

His teeth, in unison with Peter's, clicked in understanding.

The white boy was jubilant.

"You've got it, again. *Yeemara* an' *Arkooloolya*. That's what we want. Now where do we get 'em?"

The bush boy turned, moving away at right angles, into the scrub. He paused, glanced over his shoulder, then moved away again.

"*Kurura,*" he said.

There was no mistaking his meaning.

"Come on, Mary," the boy hissed excitedly. "*Kurura*. That means 'follow me.' "

He trotted eagerly after the bush boy.

Slowly, almost reluctantly, the girl followed.

After a while they came to a forest of eucalyptus. Beneath the close-woven foliage the shade was deep; a striking contrast to the glare of the bush. The white children moved uncertainly, stumblingly, their sun-narrowed pupils slow to adjust themselves to the sudden darkness. But the bush boy, his eyes refocusing almost at once, pushed quickly on. The others, stumbling and tripping over ground roots, were hard put to keep up with him.

It was cool under the gums, cool and quiet and motionless as a sylvan stage set. Hour after hour the bush boy led them on, gliding like a bar of shadow among the giant trees. He moved without apparent effort, yet quickly enough for Peter to be forced to jog-trot. Soon the small boy was panting. In spite of the shade, sweat plastered back his hair, trickled round his eyes and into his mouth. He started to lag behind. Seeing him in trouble, Mary also dropped back, and Peter reached for her hand.

The girl was pleased, gratified that in his difficulties he'd turned to her. Subconscious twinges of jealousy had been tormenting her. She had been hurt more deeply than she cared to admit at his so quickly transferring his sense of reliance from her to the bush boy. But now things were returning to normal; now he was coming back to the sisterly fold.

"All right, Peter," she whispered, "we won't leave you behind."

She knew that he must—like her—be suffering cruelly from thirst, hunger and physical exhaustion, knew that his mouth, like hers, must feel as if it were crammed with hot cotton wool. But there was nothing they could do about it. Or would it, she wondered, help if they acted like dogs—lolled out their tongues and panted?

Ahead of them the eucalyptus ended abruptly. One moment they were groping forward in deep shade, the next they were looking out across an expanse of glaring sand: mile after shimmering mile of ridge and dune, salt pan and iron rock: the Sturt Desert: heat-hazed, sun-drenched, waterless.

"*Kurura*," the bush boy said.

He started to walk into the desert.

Mary held back. She didn't exactly mistrust the bush boy, didn't doubt that if he wished he could—eventually—lead them to food and water. But how far away would the food and water be? Too far, most likely, for them ever to reach it. She sank to her knees in the shade of the last of the ghost gums. Peter collapsed beside her; the sweat from his hair ran damply into the lap of her dress.

The bush boy came back. He spoke softly, urgently, the pitch of his words rising and falling like the murmur of waves on a sandy shore. The words themselves were meaningless, but his gestures spoke plainly enough. If they stayed where they were they would die; the bush boy fell to the sand, his fingers scrabbling the dry earth. Soon the evil spirits would come to molest their bodies; the bush boy's eyes rolled in terror. But if they followed him he would take them to water; the bush boy swallowed and gulped. They hadn't far to go, only as far as the hill-that-had-fallen-out-of-the-moon; his finger pointed to a strange outcrop of rock that rose like a gargantuan cairn out of the desert, a cairn the base of which was circled by a dark, never-moving shadow.

It looked very far away.

The girl wiped the sweat out of her eyes. In the shade of the ghost-gums it was mercifully cool; far cooler than it would be in the desert. It would be so much easier, she thought, to give the struggle up, simply to stay where they were. She looked at the cairn critically. How could the bush boy know there was water there? Whoever heard of finding water on top of a pile of rock in the middle of a desert?

"Arkooloola," the bush boy insisted. He said it again and again, pointing to the base of the cairn.

The girl looked more closely, shading her eyes against the glare of the sun. She noticed that there was something strange about the shadow at the foot of the cairn. As far as she could see, it went all the way around. It couldn't, then, be ordinary shadow, caused by the sun. What else, she wondered, could create such a circle of shade? The answer came suddenly, in a flood of excitement. It must be vegetation—trees and bushes, thick, luxuriant, verdant and lush. And such vegetation, she knew, could only spring from continually-watered roots. She struggled to her feet.

It seemed a very long way to the hill-that-had-fallen-out-of-the-moon. By the time they got there the sun was setting.

They came to the humble bushes first, the twitching, quivering leaves tumbling to the sand as they approached. Then came the straw-like mellowbane, and growing amongst them grass of a very different kind—sturdy reed-thick grass, each blade tipped with a black, bean-shaped nodule: rustling death rattle, astir in the sunset wind. The bush boy snapped off one of the reeds. He drove it into the sand. Its head, when he pulled it out, was damp. He smiled encouragement.

"Arkooloola," he said, and hurried on.

The base of the cairn rose steeply, stratum upon stratum of terraced iron rock rising sheer from the desert floor; and the bottom belt was moss-coated and glistening damp, with lacy maidenhair and filigree spider fern trailing from every crevice. The children stumbled on, brushing aside the umbrella ferns, spurred forward now by the plash of water and by a sudden freshness in the air.

Peter had been lagging behind—for the last mile Mary had been half-carrying, half-dragging him. But now, like an iron filing drawn to a magnet, he broke loose and went scurrying ahead. He disappeared into the shade of the umbrella ferns, and a second later Mary heard his hoarse, excited shout.

"It's water, Mary! Water."

"Arkooloola." The bush boy grinned.

Together, black boy and white girl pushed through the tangle of fern until they came to a tiny pear-shaped basin carved out of solid rock by the ceaseless drip of water. Beside the basin Peter was flat on his face, his head, almost up to his ears, dunked in the clear translucent pool. In a second Mary was flat out beside him. Both children drank, and drank, and drank.

The water was lukewarm, for though the sun was no longer shining on it directly, the all-pervading heat had found it out and warmed it almost to the temperature of blood. As the girl drank she saw, out of the corner of her eye, the bush boy settle down beside her. She noticed that he didn't drink from the surface, but reached down, with his fingers outspread, to scoop water from the bottom of the pool. Quick to learn, she too reached down to the rocky bottom. At once the warm surface water was replaced by a current of surprising coolness: a delicious eddy from depths that the rays of the sun had never plumbed. Nectar, with a coolness doubly stimulating, doubly good.

The bush boy drank only a little. Soon he got to his feet, climbed a short way up the cairn and settled himself on a ledge of rock. Warm in the rays of the setting sun, he watched the strangers with growing curiosity. Not only, he decided, were they freakish in appearance and clumsy in movement, they were also amazingly helpless, untaught, unskilled, utterly incapable of fending for themselves—perhaps the last survivors of some peculiarly backward tribe. Unless he looked after them, they would die. That was certain. He looked at the children critically, but there was in his appraisal no suggestion of scorn. It was his peoples' way to accept individuals as they were: to help, not to criticize, the sick, the blind and the maimed.

He noticed that the smaller of the pair had finished drinking now and was climbing awkwardly toward him. He leaned down and hauled him on to the ledge of rock.

The water had revived a good deal of Peter's vitality.
He was coming now to do something that his sister
couldn't bring herself to do: to beg for food. His eyes
were on the baby wallaby, still held in the bush boy's
hand. He reached out and touched it; tentatively;
questioningly.

"Eat?" he said. *"Yeemara?"*

The sun was setting as the boys clambered down from
the rock. Twilight in the Northern Territory is short. In
half an hour it would be quite dark.

The bush boy moved quickly. Skirting the outcrop of
rock, he came to a place where a chain of billabongs
went looping into the desert—a skein of baby pools, fed
from the water hole's overflowing breast. Beside the last
of the billabongs was an area of soft sandstone rock: flat,
featureless and devoid of vegetation. Here, the bush boy
decided, was the site for their fire. He started to clear the
area of leaves, twigs and grass; everything inflammable
he swept aside so that the evil spirits of the bush fire
should have nothing to feed on.

Peter watched him: inquisitive, imitative. Soon he too
started to brush away the leaves and pull out the blades
of grass. And as he worked he fired off questions, his
chirpy falsetto echoing shrilly among the rocks.

"What are you trying to do? What are you sweepin'
the rock for like it was a rug?"

The bush boy grinned; he'd guessed what the small
one wanted to know. On the palm of his hand he placed a
dried leaf and a fragment of resin-soaked yacca wood;
then he blew on them gently, carefully, as though he
were coaxing a reluctant flame.

"Larana," he said.

"I get it!" Peter was jubilant. "You're going to light a fire."

"Larana," the bush boy insisted.

"O.K., *larana* then. You're going to light a *larana.* I'll help."

He buckled to, pouncing on bits of debris like a hungry chicken pecking at scattered corn. The bush boy clicked his teeth in approval.

From the edge of the pool Mary watched them. Again she felt a stab of jealousy, mingled this time with envy. She tried to fight it, told herself it was wrong to feel this way. But the jealousy wouldn't die. She sensed the magnetic call of boy to boy, and felt left out, alone. If only she too had been a boy! She lay quietly, face downward on the rocks, chin in hands, watching.

Peter followed the bush boy slavishly, copying his every move. Together, with sharp flints, they scooped a hollow out of the sandstone, about three feet square and nine inches deep. Then they started to forage for wood. They found it in plenty along the fringe of the desert. Yacca-yaccas: their tall, eight-foot poles, spear-straight, rising out of the middle of every tuffet of grass. The bush boy wrenched out the older poles, those that were dry and brittle with the saplessness of age. Then, among the roots, he foraged for resin—the exuded sap which had overflowed from and run down the yaccas' stems in the days of their prime. This resin was dry and waxlike, easily combustible; nature's ready-made firelighter.

Following the bush boy's example, Peter wrenched off the smaller poles and hunted assiduously for resin.

Then came the snapping of the wood into burnable fragments and the grinding of the resin into a gritty powder; then the collecting of stones (not the moisture-impregnated rock from around the billabongs—which was liable to explode when heated—but the flat, flinty and saucer-shaped stones of the desert). And at last the preparations were finished; the fire was ready to be lit.

The bush boy selected a large, smooth-surfaced chip, cut a groove along its center, then placed it in the hollow in the sandstone. Next he took a slender stem of yacca and settled the end of it into the groove of the chip. The chip was then covered with wood splinters and sprinkled with resin. Placing an open palm on either side of the yacca stem, the bush boy rubbed his hands together. Slowly at first, then faster and faster, the stem revolved in the groove, creating first friction, then heat.

As the sun sank under the rim of the desert, a spiral of woodsmoke rose thin into the evening air.

The bush boy's hands twisted faster. This was the skill that raised him above the level of the beasts. Bird can call to bird, and animal to animal; mother dingoes can sacrifice themselves for their young; termites can live in highly-organized communal towns. But they can't make fire. Man alone can harness the elements.

A blood-red glow suffused the resin. The glow spread, brightened, burst into flame. The boys piled on the sticks of yacca. The fire was made.

The bush boy collected the wallaby, held it by tail-tip over the flames, scorched it down to the bare skin. Then he laid it in the hollow. After a while he picked up a stick and started to lever the fire-heated stones on top of the carcass. Then he banked up the hollow with sand and ash. The rock wallaby baked gently.

An hour later they were eating it, watched by a single dingo and a pale, thin crescent moon. It skinned easily;

the flesh was succulent and tender; and there was enough for all.

Before they settled down to sleep the bush boy scattered the fire, stamped out every spark and smoothed out every heap of ash. Then, like a blackstone sentinel, he stood for a while beside the loop of the billabongs gazing into the desert, interpreting sounds that the children couldn't even hear. Eventually, satisfied that all was well, he lay down close to the others on the slab of sandstone rock.

A veil of cumulus drifted over the moon.

After a while the dingo crept out of the bush and on to the ledge of sandstone; warily he nosed through the ashes for bones, but he found none. A pair of flying foxes flip-flapped down to the billabong. Little folds of mist moved softly round the hill-that-had-fallen-out-of-the-moon. And the children slept.

CHAPTER SEVEN

The girl woke early, in the whiteness and stillness of the false dawn, in the hour before sunrise when the light is very clear and the earth peculiarly still. She lay on her back, watching the stars die and the sky pale. Was heaven there, she wondered, somewhere beyond stars and sky? If it hadn't been for the bush boy, she'd probably know by now. She rolled onto her side and looked at the naked Aboriginal, then looked quickly away. If only she, too, had been a boy!

She tried to think calmly and logically. One thing she was certain of: the bush boy had saved their lives. He was used to living in the desert. That was obvious. So long as they stayed with him they'd probably keep alive. But they'd still be lost. Could they, she wondered, persuade him to take them all the way to Adelaide? But perhaps he didn't know where Adelaide was. . . . She wondered what he was doing, wandering the desert alone, far from family or tribe. It was all very puzzling.

A few weeks ago she'd have known what to do, known what was best. But here in the desert most of the old rules and the old values seemed strangely meaningless. Uncertain, unsure, she fell back on a woman's oldest line of action—passivity. She'd simply wait and see.

The decision brought immediate relief. Now she'd

relinquished her leadership and all its implied responsibility, much of her keyed-up tension ebbed away. Rolling on to her back she closed her eyes and fell almost at once into a deep refreshing sleep.

She woke a couple of hours later to the sound of laughter and splashing water. Sitting up, she saw her brother and the black boy bathing in the billabong. They were ducking each other beneath a miniature waterfall that cascaded down from the rock.

"Come on, Mary," her brother shouted. "In with us."

"Come on, Mary," the rocks reechoed. "In with us. In with us."

She waved cheerfully.

"Later," she shouted. "When it's warmer."

Peter opened his mouth to remonstrate, but his mouth filled suddenly with water; the bush boy had ducked him again. Peter flailed his arms. Like a miniature waterspout he rushed his assailant. The bush boy feigned defeat; in mock terror he fled across the billabong. Splashing through the shallows, still pursued by Peter, he clambered onto the farther bank. There he paused. Even in play, part of his attention had been subconsciously focused on the ever-present problem of survival, the never satisfied search for food. Now, close to the billabong, he started to probe at a cluster of bulb-shaped protuberances in the sand. With his long prehensile toes he scratched away the topsoil, uncovering a soft, brown-skinned ball, about the size of a coconut.

"Worwora!" his voice was excited.

Peter came scrambling out of the water. Doubtfully, he looked at the ball; hopefully, he touched it.

"Yeemara?" he asked.

The bush boy nodded, and together they started to unearth the strange coconut ball. It was one of nature's paradoxes: a plant growing upside down, a leaf and flower-bearing liana whose foliage grew entirely under the ground. Close to the surface was the tuber-like root; spread out around and beneath it were its flowers and leaves, drawing from the soil that sustenance which the air of the desert denied. It was a plant as rare as it was strange, and as tasty as it looked unpalatable.

The bush boy broke off the yamlike root; then, following another skein of underground foliage, he tracked down a second. Fascinated, Peter watched. He got the idea quickly. Soon he too had sought out and pulled up a third *worwora*. The bush boy grinned in appreciation. The little one was quick to learn. Following the lines of underground foliage, the two boys worked gradually away from the billabong. Soon, side by side, they disappeared into the desert.

When they were out of sight Mary came down to the chain of pools. Soon she too was laughing and splashing under the waterfall. But she listened carefully for sound of the boys' return. As soon as she heard their voices, she scrambled out of the water and quickly pulled on her dress.

The boys' arms were full of *worworas*. They were carrying at least a dozen each; and they were, Mary suddenly noticed, both of them quite naked. She picked up her brother's shorts from beside the edge of the billabong.

"Peter," she said, "come here."

He came reluctantly across.

"Gosh, I don't need clothes, Mary. It's too hot."

"Put them on," she said.

He recognized her strict mother's voice.

A week ago he wouldn't have dreamed of arguing. But somehow he felt different here in the desert. He looked at his sister defiantly, weighing the odds of revolt.

"O.K.," he said at last. "I'll wear the shorts. But nothing else."

A week ago the girl wouldn't have stood for conditions. But somehow, for her too, things were different now. She accepted the compromise without complaint.

They cooked the yamlike roots in the reheated ash of last night's fire. They tasted good: sweet and pulpy, a cross between potato, artichoke and parsnip.

During the meal Mary watched the black boy. They owed him their lives. His behavior was impeccable. He looked healthy and scrupulously clean. All this she admitted. Yet his nakedness still appalled her. She felt guilty every time she looked at him. If only he, like Peter, would wear a pair of shorts! She told herself that it wasn't his fault he was naked, that his nakedness was due, purely and simply, to his primitive way of life. But this didn't make it, for her, any more acceptable. If only, she thought, they could rustle up another pair of shorts. . . .

The idea came to her suddenly, like an inspiration. And while the boys were scattering ash from the fire, she moved to the far side of the cairn, hitched up her dress and stepped out of her pants.

Then she walked across to the bush boy and touched him on the shoulder. She felt both compassion and satisfaction, as, like a dignitary bestowing some supremely

precious gift, she handed her pants to the naked
Aboriginal.

He took them shyly; wondering, not knowing what
they were for. He put the *worwora* down and examined
the gift more closely. His fingers explored the elastic top.
Its flick-back was something he didn't yet fully
understand. (Bark thread and liana vine didn't behave
like this.) He stretched the elastic taut, tested it,
experimented with it, was trying to unravel it when Peter
came to his aid.

"Hey, don't undo 'em. Put 'em on. One foot in here,
one foot in there. Then pull them up."

The words were meaningless to the bush boy, but the
small one's miming was clear enough. He was cautious
at first, suspicious of letting himself be hobbled. Yet his
instinct told him that the strangers meant him no harm,
that their soft, barklike offering was a gift, a token of
gratitude. It would be impolite to refuse. Helped by
Peter, he climbed carefully into the pants.

Mary sighed with relief. Decency had been restored.

But Peter looked at the bush boy critically. There was
something wrong, something incongruous. He couldn't
spot the trouble at first. Then, quite suddenly, he saw it:
the border of intricately woven lace. He tried his hardest
not to laugh; his sister, he knew, wouldn't approve of his
laughing. He clapped a hand to his mouth, but it was no
good; it had to come. Like a baby kookaburra he
exploded suddenly into a shrill and unmelodious cackle.
Then, giving way to uninhibited delight, he started to
caper around and around the bush boy. His finger shot
out.

"Look! Look! He's got lacy panties on. Sissy girl!
Sissy girl! Sissy girl!"

Faster and faster he whirled his mocking fandango.

Mary was horrified. But for the bush boy, Peter's antics supplied the half-expected cue. He knew for certain now why the strange gift had been made, knew what it signified—the prelude to a jamboree, the dressing up that heralded the start of a ritual dance. The little one had started the dancing; now it was up to him to keep it going. He did so with wholehearted zest.

The joyful caperings of Peter were nothing compared to the contortions the bush boy now went into. He leaped and bounded around the billabong with the abandon of a dervish run amok. It was a symbolic combat he danced, a combat in which he was both victor and vanquished, a combat between life and death. He had no emu feathers in his hair, no moistened ocher streaking his face and chest; but he snatched up a stem of yacca wood for spear and a splinter of ironbark for club, and jabbing, dodging, feinting and parrying he fought his pantomime self to exhaustion. It was the tribal dance he enjoyed most, the war dance, the natural and inevitable sequel to dressing up.

Brother and sister watched his act, first in amazement, then in unrestrained delight.

Kup, kup, yurr-rr-rra! Kup, kup, kurr-rr-rra!

The bush boy's war cry started like the yap of an attacking dingo and ended in the bush dog's throat-shaking growl. He became utterly lost in his battle; the pantomime became reality. First he was the triumphant attacker; in and out the yacca wood darted like the jab of a fish-barbed spear; round and about the ironbark flailed, battering, parrying, crushing. Then he transferred himself to the receiving end. He clutched at his chest, wrenching out the imagined fish-barbs; he smote his forehead, smashing himself to the sand; dazedly he staggered up. But with an ear-splitting howl of victory his assailant was on him. The spear stabbed through his heart. With a choking cry the defeated warrior toppled from the crest of a sand dune; in a grotesque, stiff-limbed somersault, he slid to the desert floor. Then he lay still. The battle was over, but the victory parade was still to come.

Like a phoenix rising, the victor sprang from the vanquished's body. His fists he clenched and knotted above his head—like a boxer self-acknowledging his prowess. His feet he pulled proudly up in a high-kicking march of victory—an ebullient, primitive goose step. And after every so many paces he leaped high into the air and brought both heels up from behind to strike himself on the buttocks with a resounding, flesh-tingling slap. At first the tempo of the victory dance was slow and measured, stylized. But gradually it quickened. The goose-stepping became higher, faster; the leaping more frenzied, more abandoned. The bush boy's body glistened with sweat. His breathing quickened. His nostrils dilated. His eyes rolled. Yet still the dance went on: ever faster, ever wilder. He was swaying now to a drumbeat that couldn't be heard, caught up in a ritual that couldn't be broken. On and on and on, though his muscles were aching, his lungs bursting, his heart pounding and his mind empty as the cloudless sky. Then suddenly the climax: somersault after somersault, victory roll after victory roll, till he was standing, stock still and in sudden silence, face to face with the children.

And once again he was naked; for at the moment of climax the elastic of the pants had snapped, and the gift—symbol of civilization—lay under his feet, trampled into the desert sand.

White girl and black boy, a couple of yards apart, stood staring one at another.

The girl's eyes grew wider and wider.

The bush boy's eyes widened too. He realized, suddenly and for the first time, that the larger of the strangers wasn't a male; she was a lubra, a budding gin.

He took a half-pace forward. Then he drew back, appalled. For into the girl's eyes there came a terror such as he had seen only a couple of times before, a terror that could for him have only one meaning, one tragic and inevitable cause. He began to tremble then, in great, uncontrolled and nerve-jerking spasms. For, to him, the girl's terror could have only one meaning: that she had seen in his eyes an image—the image of the Spirit of Death.

CHAPTER EIGHT

To the bush boy everything had its appointed time. There was a time to be weaned, a time to be carried in arms; a time to walk with the tribe, a time to walk alone; a time for the proving-of-manhood, a time for the taking of gins; a time for hunting and a time to die. These times were preordained. They never overlapped. A boy couldn't walk before he'd been weaned; couldn't take a gin before his manhood had been proved. These things were done in order.

This was why the question of the girl's sex had never interested the bush boy; didn't, indeed, interest him now. For in his tribal timetable he had only arrived at the stage of walking alone, the stage immediately preceding the proving-of-manhood, the stage of the walkabout.

In the bush boy's tribe every male who reached the age of thirteen or fourteen had to perform a walkabout—a selective test which weeded out and exterminated the weaker members of the tribe and ensured that only the fittest survived to father children. This custom is not common to all Aboriginal tribes, but is confined to the most primitive and least known of the Aboriginal groups who live among the water holes of the Central and North Australian desert. The test consisted of journeying from one group of water holes to another; a journey which took some six to eight months and was made entirely unaided and alone. It was a test of mental and physical toughness far fairer—but no less rigorous—than the Spartan exposure of newborn babes.

It was this test that the bush boy was now engaged on. He had been doing well, had covered the most difficult part of the journey. Yet he wasn't, it seemed, to be allowed to finish it. For the lubra had looked into his eyes and seen the Spirit of Death.

Death was the Aboriginal's only enemy, his only fear. There was for him no future life, no Avalon, no Valhalla, no Islands of the Blest. That perhaps was why he watched for death with such unrelaxing vigilance; that certainly was why he feared it with a terror beyond all "civilized" comprehension. That was why he now stood in the middle of the Sturt Plain, trembling and ice-cold, his body beaded in little globules of sweat.

Peter looked in amazement, first at the bush boy then at his sister. He couldn't grasp what was happening; couldn't understand how things had gone so suddenly and terribly wrong. Afraid, his recently acquired confidence fast draining away, he reached for his sister's hand. Then, unexpectedly, he started to cry.

To the bush boy the little one's tears were confirmation; confirmation of what the lubra had seen. He turned away. He left the *worwora* at the edge of the billabong; he left the lace-edged pants by the ashes of last night's hearth. Slowly he walked away, into the desert.

CHAPTER NINE

The children watched him. The girl was pale and breathing quickly. The boy was whimpering; shocked, frightened, caught up in a cross fire of emotions he couldn't begin to understand. But one fact did penetrate the haze of his bewilderment. The bush boy, for the second time since their meeting him, was deserting them. Their lifeline, once again, was drifting away.

Suddenly and violently, he flung off his sister's hand and rushed stumbling into the desert.

"Come back!" His voice was frightened. "Come back. Come back."

The bush boy walked on, unheeding, apparently unhearing, like a sleepwalker. But Peter wouldn't be denied. Blindly he launched himself at the bush boy's legs, clutching him round the knees.

"You're not to go," he panted.

And he hung on, like a leech.

The bush boy was jerked to a halt, was shaken out of his trance. He put his hands on the white boy's shoulders, pushing him gently away. But Peter wouldn't release his grip.

"You're not going." He repeated it over and over again. "Not going. Not going. Not going."

The bush boy squatted down, so that his face was close

to the little one's, so that the little one could look into his eyes and see the terrible thing that was there. With their faces less than eighteen inches apart the two boys stared into each other's eyes.

But to the bush boy's astonishment, the little one didn't draw back; gave no exclamation of terror; seemed to see nothing wrong. He got to his feet. Puzzled. For a moment hope came surging back. Perhaps the lubra had been mistaken; perhaps the Spirit of Death had been only passing through him, resting awhile as he passed from one tribe to another; perhaps he had left him now.

He retraced his steps, back toward the girl.

But as soon as he neared her, hope drained away. For at his approach the lubra again shrank back; in her eyes all the former terror came welling up.

The bush boy knew then that he was going to die. Not perhaps today, nor tomorrow, nor even the next day. But soon. Before the coming of the rains and the smoking of spirits out of the tribal caves. This knowledge numbed his mind, but didn't paralyze it. He was still able to think of other things. Of the queer strangers, for example—the lubra and the little one—of what would happen to them. When he died, they would die too. That was certain, for they were such helpless creatures. So there'd be not one victim for the Spirit of Death but three. Unless he could somehow save them?

It seemed, on the face of it, an impossible undertaking. With a stem of yacca he traced a pattern in the sand: circle after circle, symbolic rings of protection against Wulgaru, the Spirit of Death. And at last, in a moment of sudden inspiration, he saw what had to be done. He must lead the strangers to safety, to the final goal of his walkabout, the valley-of-waters-under-the-earth. And they must waste no time. For who knew how much time they would have.

He gathered up the *worwora* and smoothed out the ash of the fire.

"*Kurura,*" he said, and struck out across the desert.

The little one followed him at once. But the lubra didn't move. He thought for a long time that she had decided to stay by the billabongs, but in the end she too started to follow, keeping a long way behind.

Mary and Peter begin their 1,400-mile trek through the Australian Outback, hampered by unrelenting sun and exhaustion.

Above:
Having come upon a waterhole, they fashion protection from the sun and fall asleep. As they sleep, they are visited by curious creatures of the desert.

Right:
Peter discovers that their water is all gone. Unless they are able to find water, the children will die.

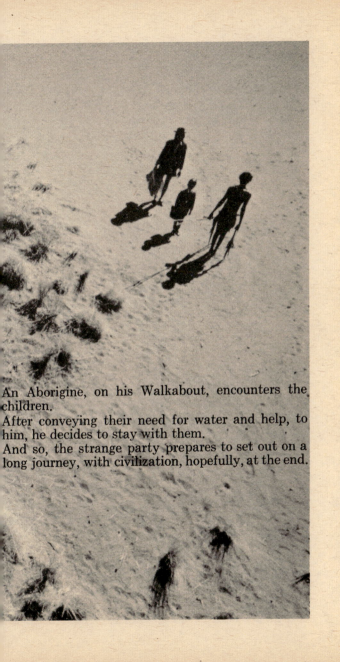

An Aborigine, on his Walkabout, encounters the children.
After conveying their need for water and help, to him, he decides to stay with them.
And so, the strange party prepares to set out on a long journey, with civilization, hopefully, at the end.

With doubt and optimism, Mary and Peter follow
their guide through the bleak North Australian
Desert.

Above And Right:
Peter, gradually, loses fear of the Aborigine and, at last, offers his prize possession, a red toy soldier, to him. Mary has mixed feelings about the bush boy.

Below Right:
Confused by these two strange creatures and by what he should do, the Aborigine withdraws to a hilltop as night comes. According to the laws of his tribe, he should not be with any other human beings while he is on his Walkabout.

But the children need help or they will surely perish! The Aborigine decides for the children and against his own loneliness.

Above:
Passing many animals, the three come upon some camels. Peter has a momentary hallucination about his father riding one of the camels, but this is the last note of their past tragedy. The future is somewhere across the desert.

Above Right:
The Aborigine takes aim to secure supper for them. No matter how empty the land seems, he is always able to find food.

Below Right:
The three settle down for the day and the Aborigine cooks his "kill"; Peter and Mary do not look forward to this kind of supper, but know that they must eat to survive.

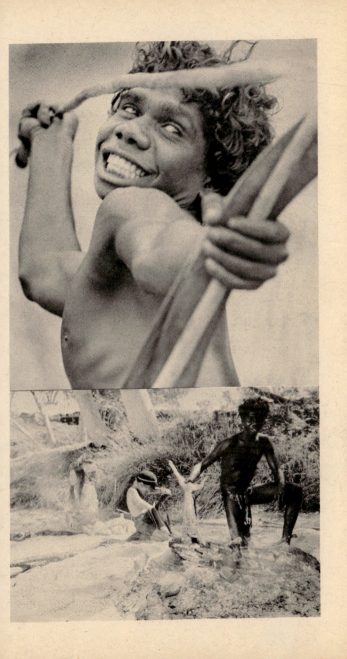

The terror and uncertainty fading, Mary and Peter
begin to be friends of the bush boy. He delights in
their company and they play in the trees. For Peter,
he is an older brother.

As the three swing from tree limbs, the Aborigine begins to look at Mary with something more than the friendship of children. And Mary becomes aware of his adult feeling.

Above:

As the three rest, Mary instinctively stays at a distance, while Peter and the Aborigine—the two men —survey the unknown land before them.

Right:

They enter a ravine of lush vegetation and cool streams. Mary and Peter are further and further from their past life as they adapt to the demands of this strange country. The Aborigine leads them to a rock wall, where he paints incredible figures on the stone and on the two children.

The three enter a grotto, where they go swimming. They are alone in the world, but it is their special world.

The Aborigine realizes that he is not and cannot be of the world of the children. He has broken his tribe's sacred traditions and has, thus, because of the rejection of the girl, lost both possible worlds. In ancient manner, he prepares himself to leave this world, to die.

CHAPTER TEN

The desert was neither flat nor monotonous; nor was it like so many other deserts—the Gobi, the Steppes, or certain parts of the Sahara—featureless and devoid of color. Its formation was varied: patches of sand, outcrops of rock, dried-up watercourses, salt pans, faults and frequent belts of sparse vegetation. And its colors were strong: bold and harsh and sharply defined, belts of yellow, blocks of bottle-green, and patches of fire-flame, red as fields of blood.

The bush boy led the way unhesitatingly; across the salt pans, through the scattered yellow jackets—poor relations to the gums—around the outcrops of quartz and granite. It was eight years since his tribe had last passed this way. He'd been little more than a toddler then; but small as he was his memory had been at work, recording landmarks and storing up information that might be of use for the future—information that was proving invaluable now.

Soon they came to a valley, gently rising, coiling like a lifeless snake aslant a range of low red hills. Here the country was sparsely timbered: stately white-barked eucalyptus, tatty yellow jackets, saw-leafed banksias and occasional patches of sandalwood—source of the incense-shedding joss sticks that smoulder beneath the images of a million oriental gods. There were more birds among the trees. There hadn't been many beside the hill-that-had-fallen-out-of-the-moon; but here, in the shade of the eucalyptus, they were present in their thousands: gang-gangs and finches, honeysuckers and soldier birds, budgerigars (lovebirds to the romantically minded; tiny flittering gems of mauve and olive, gold, jade-green and cobalt-blue) and, perched on the branches of the gum tree, row after row of wonga-wongas: sad-faced, motionless, silent as the desert itself.

After the children had pushed some way into the valley, another type of bird made its presence known: a strange, sorrowful bird that followed their tracks, hopping from branch to branch with piteous, heart-rending cries.

"It isn't yours," he wailed. "It isn't yours."

The children paused; looked back. At first they could see nothing. Then, with a sudden fluttering swoop, a red-breasted pardalote swept over their heads to settle on the branch of a nearby eucalyptus.

"It isn't yours. It isn't yours." The mournful cry echoed among the leaves.

The bush boy turned to Peter, explaining by mime the pardalote's behavior. Ahead was water—thirstily the bush boy gulped—where the bird was accustomed to drink; and he was loath to share his private reservoir with strangers. For the pardalote was a bird with an abnormal thirst; he drank eighty to a hundred times a day, and not by the normal process of imbibing through the beak, but by settling himself on top of the water, spreading his wings and absorbing liquid through the delicate membrane of his skin. No wonder he wanted to keep his pool to himself! Yet by his very loquaciousness he sometimes guided others to the water he sought to hide. The bush boy led on, knowing that should he take a wrong turn the pardalote's contented silence would warn him of his mistake. And soon they came to a small, fern-ringed water hole, fed by an underground spring.

The pardalote, by now, had stopped his wailing. In angry silence he watched the children drinking his water, refreshing themselves at his pool.

It was midday. The sun was hot; and the boys scooped up great palmfuls of water and sloshed them over their heads. Mary too. But she wouldn't go near the bush boy; and whenever he looked at her, she shrank away.

For lunch they ate the *worwora*—uncooked.

During the meal Peter tried to comfort his sister: asked her what she was frightened of. But he soon gave up. She was he decided, in one of her incomprehensible moods. Girls were like that. Sometimes the only thing to do was to leave them alone. He wandered across to the bush boy and lay down beside him, in the shade of an outcrop of rock.

They stayed by the pool for three hours, avoiding the worst of the heat; then the bush boy decided it was time they moved on. And soon they were again on their way, traversing the upper slopes of the gently sloping valley.

They covered fifteen miles that day. The bush boy could have walked twice as far. But Peter tired easily; and the Aboriginal adjusted his pace accordingly. Also Peter had lost his shoes—having left them together with his shirt somewhere beside the billabongs—and his feet, unused to the hard going, had started to blister.

Late in the evening they came to the head of the valley, to where it petered out on the edge of a million-acre plateau. The trees were still with them, though not so thickly growing now. So were the birds. The chat-chats, the corellas and the sweetly singing bell-birds; and, a little before dark, the bustards. There were three of the bustards. Foolish, inquisitive birds, rather like scraggy turkeys, they followed the children almost at their heels: sniffing, scratching and pecking. The bush boy watched them thoughtfully, calculating their food value. One was smaller than the others, the chick; he would be tender, and plump enough to satisfy the hunger of three. Slowly, imperceptibly, the bush boy dropped behind, edging ever closer to the foolish birds, Suddenly—as if it had been thrown—his hand flew out. His fingers closed around the baby bustard's neck; cut off its life in a single twisting jerk.

Swinging his victim carelessly, the bush boy went up to the girl. Before she realized quite what was happening, he had thrust the bustard, wings and body still a-twitch, into her arms. For wasn't she a lubra, a carrier of burdens?

Blood from the broken neck splashed darkly on to the girl's dress. But she didn't drop the bustard. She held on to it, tightly, though her face puckered in nausea with every twitch of its wings.

Peter saw her distress.

"Poor old Mary! He should have given it to me. I'll carry it for you."

He tried to take hold of the bird, but the girl turned away.

"It's heavy," she whispered. "I'll take it."

In single file they pushed on, over the rim of the plateau, ebony silhouettes against a sunset sky.

That night they camped in a fault, a broad slab-sided rift that split the plateau like a crack in sun-dried mud.

There was no water; but the rocks retained the warmth of the sun, and the twilight wind passed high over their heads.

The bush boy again made fire, though this time there was little yacca wood, and it proved more difficult to light. But by the time the sun had set, flames were flickering cheerfully, their shadows were duplicated on the firelit rocks of the fault, and by the time the Southern Cross had tilted up, low on the horizon, the bustard was cooking in the fire-heated ash. They would eat it, the bush boy indicated, in the morning.

As they lay down to sleep, all the day's constraint—which had ebbed somewhat away during the lighting of the fire—came flooding back. The girl kept moving about, keeping the fire between herself and the bush boy. Peter, worn out by the day's exertions, quite lost patience with her.

"Stop fidgeting, Mary!" His voice was peevish. "I can't get to sleep."

"Sorry, Pete."

For a while there was silence. The bush boy moved quietly about the camp, banking down the fire, brushing aside random splinters of wood. Watching him, the girl tossed and turned. At last she could bear it no longer.

"Peter!" Her voice was low, and somehow different from usual. Pleading, almost frightened.

"Yes?"

"Come and lie close to me. Please."

"What for?"

"I'm cold."

Reluctantly he crawled across, and the two children snuggled closely together.

The girl insisted on lying with her face to the fire.

From where she lay she could see the bush boy, silhouetted against the firelight; he was standing on one foot, staring into the moonlit valley. She wondered what he was thinking, wondered if he was waiting for her to fall asleep. But I won't sleep, she promised herself. Not till he does. She said it over and over again. Not till he does. Not till he does. But at last her eyes started to droop, her breathing to deepen; and a little before midnight, in spite of her resolutions, she slept the sleep of the utterly exhausted.

But the bush boy didn't sleep. Hour after hour he stood there, silent, motionless, a shadow carved in ebony and moonlight.

CHAPTER ELEVEN

Physically the Australian Aboriginal is tough. He can stand any amount of heat, exposure or cold, and his incidence to pain is remarkably low. But he has his Achilles' Heel, mental euthanasia, a propensity for dying purely of autosuggestion.

Experiments have proved this—experiments carried out by Australia's leading doctors. On the one hand a group of Aboriginals—voluntarily of course—have spent a day in the desert at a temperature of roughly 95°-100° Fahrenheit, and have then spent the night in a sealed-off chamber, thermostatically controlled to a temperature of minus 15° (47° of frost). They slept well without any sort of protection, and, though they were naked, felt no cold. On the other hand, Aboriginals who are 100 percent physically fit have been known to die purely because a tribal medicine man has put the death curse on them. One such man was admitted to a state-capital hospital. Thorough tests proved that there was nothing the matter with him; psychoanalysts tried to instill in him the desire to fight and the will to live. But in vain. The medicine man had said he was going to die. And die he did, of self-induced apathy.

Death, to the Aboriginal, is something that can't be fought. Those whom the Spirit wants, he takes; and it's no good kicking against the pricks.

That was why the bush boy accepted the fact of his impending death without question and without struggle. There was in his mind no flicker of hope. The lubra's terror, to him, could have only the one meaning. He had seen terror like hers before: in a woman's eyes after prolonged and unsuccessful childbirth; in an old man's face when he had become too weak to walk and the tribe had passed him by, leaving him alone in the waterless desert. And so he now stood, without hope, passively waiting; wondering, as he stared across the moonlit valley, how and when the Spirit of Death would come to claim him.

CHAPTER TWELVE

All night the bustard baked in the ashes, and by morning it was tender as broiled lamb. The children ate it hungrily.

Peter and Mary wanted to linger over the meal, would have liked to pick every succulent scrap off the bustard's bones, but the bush boy was impatient to be off. Morning mist was still clinging to the sides of the rift valley when he smoothed out the ashes of the fire, beckoned to the others and moved off along the fault. He set a fast pace.

Mary, not knowing the cause of his hurry, wished he'd be more considerate, for Peter's sake. But, in spite of her misgivings, Peter's vitality—at least in the early morning—seemed to be limitless, quite capable of measuring up to the bush boy's loping stride. Indeed, he apparently had energy to spare. For he hopped around the bush boy like an exuberant puppy, his shrill questioning voice echoing back from the rocks. And strangely enough the Aboriginal seemed to be understanding—and answering—his questions.

Peter had decided to learn the black boy's language—it would be far more useful than the French his sister was always so proud of. He trotted up to the Aboriginal, holding a fragment of rock.

"What's the name for this?"

"*Garsha.*" The bush boy spoke with a grating harshness, hard as the flint itself.

"And this?" The white boy plucked a tussock of grass.

"*Karathara.*" The word was whispered, liltingly, like the rustle of wind through a sea of grain.

"*Garsha. Karathara . . . Garsha. Karathara,*" Peter's reedy treble echoed down the valley. He went rushing on ahead. Presently he came trotting back and handed the bush boy a lump of quartz. Hour after hour the questioning went on. Mary felt very much alone.

For lunch they ate yams, queer-looking bushman-drakes that grew in disheveled heaps beneath an outcrop of rock. Once again they rested through the midday heat—at least Mary rested; the boys chattered like gossiping kookaburras—then they were walking again, heading southwest across the dull-red sandstone plateau.

The plateau was not a pleasant place for walking. It shimmered with heat; the children's footsteps kicked up a cloud of fine red dust, and there was no water. Soon even the ebullient Peter was reduced to a sober plod. The dust hung for a long time in the air, so that the children, looking back, could see behind them a winding haze of redness stretching far across the plain. After a while Peter started to sneeze. The dust was tickling his nose.

At the first sneeze the bush boy grinned (remembering their original meeting); but when the sneezing continued, becoming louder and louder as the dust inflamed Peter's nostrils, the bush boy looked at him anxiously. He hoped the little one hadn't caught the fever-that-comes-with-the-rains.

Peter, in fact, was starting nothing worse than a common cold—the type that is almost chronic among people who fly long distances and experience sudden changes in temperature—and this cold was now being aggravated by the plateau dust. He sneezed and sneezed and sneezed; he went red in the face, and his eyes poured water. The bush boy regarded him with astonishment. Aboriginals know all about fever, but they never have colds and they seldom sneeze. Certainly the black boy had never witnessed such prolonged and noisy paroxysms as Peter's.

All that afternoon and half the evening the little boy sneezed his way across the dusty plain; he only stopped when they came to the edge of the plateau and the soft redstone gave way to granite, smooth and hard, not to be kicked up by shuffling feet. By the time they stopped for the night Peter was utterly exhausted. Too tired to help the bush boy with fire-making, and too worn-out to eat, he crawled wearily across to his sister, put his head on her lap and fell instantly asleep.

The bush boy banked down the fire. He was pleased with their progress—that day they had covered seventeen miles. If they kept to this pace, another seven sleeps would see them to the valley-of-waters-under-the-earth. Once they reached it, the strangers would be safe.

He didn't go near the lubra, knowing that for some reason his nearness alarmed her (perhaps because she was ignorant enough to think that the Spirit of Death might pass, in juxtaposition, from him to her). Instead, he lay quietly down, on the opposite side of the fire. He was about to drift quietly into the dreamtime when, unexpectedly, he sneezed.

Morning mist refracted the rays of the sun, tumbling them into the valley like a river of burning cold. Bathed in sudden light, the children stirred.

The bush boy was first to wake. He woke completely and instantly, every bit of him together: one second lost to the world, the next completely alert. He rose, flexed his muscles, sniffed the air and walked quietly down-valley.

Peter woke next. He sat up yawning, rubbing eyes and nose. He'd have liked to blow his nose really (it felt all bunged-up), but having no handkerchief, he sniffed, loudly.

His sister rolled onto her side and looked at him critically.

"Peter." Her voice was disapproving. "Where's your handkerchief?"

"Lost."

He didn't wait for recriminations, but got up quickly.

"I'm going to look for the bush boy. Coming?"

She shook her head and lay down again. He wondered why she looked suddenly hurt, as though he'd slapped her across the face.

He wandered off, hands in pockets, sniffing loudly.

Instinctively he headed down-valley, through the broad granite cleft which ran like an axe-cut from the rim of the plateau to the fringe of the plain. He had been too tired the night before to take much notice of their campsite—it had been simply a place to go to sleep in; but now, the scenery's bizarre grandeur caught his imagination. It was, he decided, just like the moon, just like the rocky, dun-colored lunar landscapes in the astronauts' pictures. He peered at the rocks a little apprehensively, half-expecting some monster-from-

another-world to come leaping out; indeed, from the far
side of a jagged outcrop of granite, he could, now that he
listened carefully, hear something that sounded rather
like a monster feeding, a sort of scrunching-mingled-
with-heavy-breathing noise. Fear fought curiosity and
lost. Cautiously he squirmed his way up the wall of rocks
and peered over the edge.

Twenty feet below him was a small pool, rock-ringed,
crystal clear and motionless as glass. And beside it was
the bush boy, trundling a small boulder of quartz about
the size of a football (but ten times its weight). He saw
Peter and grinned.

"Yarrawa!" He pointed to the pool.

Peter glissaded down. He saw the *yarrawa* at
once—fish: silver-scaled, glistening, darting; ranging in
size from three to fifteen inches; on their sides a row of
small black dots, like the portholes of a liner. He
suddenly remembered that he'd had no breakfast.

"Yeemara?" He pointed at the fish.

The bush boy nodded.

The pool was shallow at one end, and Peter waded in.
He could see the fish quite clearly; there were thousands
of them—well, hundreds, anyhow—but whenever his
hand snaked down to clutch them, they darted away like
quicksilver. The bush boy laughed. He beckoned Peter
out of the pool and led him to a smooth circular rock,
smaller than his, but quite as heavy, he suspected, as the
little one could lift.

"Kurura," he said, and started to trundle his boulder
of quartz up to a shelving ledge of rock that overhung the
pool. Peter followed him; and soon the boys and their
stones were poised on the edge of the rock which jutted
out, like a diving board, over the water. The bush boy

mimed his intention. Peter nodded in understanding; and together they hoisted up their boulders, staggered with them to the lip of the rock and hurled them into the pool. The splash was cataclysmic, loud as a whipcrack, echoing around the encircling rock; the spray was torrential, like the collapsing of a miniature waterspout; and the concussion, in the confined, rockbound pool, was overwhelming, like the explosion of a depth charge. The fish were stunned. Upside down, they came floating to the surface.

The bush boy leaped into the pool. Peter followed. Together, they grabbed the paralyzed fish and tossed them out of the water, onto the rocks. Within sixty seconds a couple of dozen *yarrawa* were squirming their lives out on the smooth, sun-hot granite.

The bush boy was jubilant. Climbing out of the pool, he gathered the fish together in a twisting, glistening heap, playing with them, trickling them through his fingers like a miser his gold.

There were so many fish and they were so slippery that when the boys wanted to take them back to the campsite they couldn't carry them—not until Peter took off his shorts. They wrapped the *yarrawa* up in them, and carried them back in triumph.

When the children had eaten—three fish apiece—Peter refused to put on his shorts. There was quite a scene.

"Feel them," the little boy said. "They're horrid and scaly. Full of fish."

"Wash them, and put them on," his sister ordered.

"Shan't!"

Peter eyed her defiantly.

It was the bush boy who settled the argument. He was

ready to move again; the *yarrawa* were too valuable to be left behind; so he rolled them up in the little one's shorts and tossed the bundle to the lubra.

"*Kurura,*" he said.

And so they began the fourth day of the walkabout.

The going was easier than on the plateau: down the lower reaches of the valley then out across the plain—the vast, lonely and limitless plain that rolled on and on, a flowering wilderness, silent as sleep, motionless as death.

Over the level ground the bush boy moved quickly. Too quickly for Peter, whose cold made him short of breath. Soon the little boy was panting. After a couple of hours his nose started to stream. The midday halt—in the shade of a group of golden casuarinas—was never more welcome. But it only lasted a couple of hours. Then they were walking again, across the endless plain, on and on.

Halfway through the afternoon, as they were crossing a monotonous belt of scrub, there came a diversion: as welcome as it was unexpected. The children were walking in their usual order—the bush boy first, Peter next, Mary in the rear—when suddenly the bush boy stopped dead, like a pointer, one foot off the ground, nose forward, an arm flung behind him for balance. For perhaps half a minute he stayed motionless, frozen; then he crept quietly forward, to where a low bank of wattle bush formed a screen around a tiny clearing. Expectantly the others joined him. Together they peered through the wattle leaves.

They saw a bird, an ordinary rather sad-looking bird, with big eyes, pointed beak and long, straggling tail. He was scratching about for grubs. To the white children the scene looked very prosaic: an anti-climax. But the black boy was obviously enthralled; he signaled them to be quiet, and so they knelt close to the wattle bushes: motionless, expectant. And after about twenty minutes their patience was rewarded.

Quite suddenly the bird raised his head; he drew himself erect and, with a stiff-legged goose step, strutted into the center of the clearing. Then he started to sing. And in an instant all his drabness was sloughed away, for his song was beautiful beyond compare: stream after stream of limpid melodious notes, flowing and mingling, trilling and soaring: bush music, magic as the pipes of Pan. On and on it went, wave after wave of perfect harmony that held the children spell-bound. At last the notes sank into a croon, died into silence. The song was over. But not the performance. For now came a metamorphosis too amazing to be believed. The drab-brown bird with its tatty, straggling tail disappeared, and in its place rose a creature of pure beauty. The drooping tail fanned wide; its two outmost feathers swung erect to form the frame of a perfect lyre; and in between spread a mist of elfin plumage, a phantasmagoria of blue and silver, shot with gold, that trembled and quivered with all the beauty of a rainbow seen through running water. Then, hidden behind its plumage, the lyre bird again burst into song. And as he sang, he danced; prancing joyfully from side to side, hopping and skipping to the beat of a high-speed polka. And every now and then his song broke off, was interspersed with croaking chuckles of happiness.

Then, as suddenly as his performance had begun, it ended. The feathers drooped, the polka came to a halt, the singing died. And he was just another bird,

The children walked on. The sun dropped lower. The western sky glowed rose and gold.

At the first breath of the sunset wind they made camp beside a group of eucalyptus. There was no water, but the fish alleviated their thirst.

Soon, out of the dusk, came the ants; winged ants, flying in swarms, attracted by the glow of the fire. Mating in midair they shed their wings, dropping intertwined to earth. The bush boy stirred up the flames to move them on. Coils of woodsmoke streamed downwind.

Peter moved farther away from the fire—for the smoke brought tears to his eyes and precipitated another attack of sneezing. But his sneezes were neither as prolonged nor as violent as they had been the night before. For his cold was on the mend. Though they had again walked close to fifteen miles, he felt reasonably fresh: fresh enough, at any rate, to appreciate the miming.

For now, out of the shadows and into the firelight, strutted the bush boy. In his hands were three small leafy branches. These he draped about his body to represent wings and tail. Then he started to dance: to mimic the polka-ing lyre bird. Around and around the fire he strutted, pantomimed and pranced; then he screwed up his mouth and burst into shrill, raucous singing. His absurdities grew more tempestuous, more abandoned, yet never lost their realism.

At first the white children were simply amused. Then, as the pantomime grew even livelier, even more grotesque, their amusement turned to unrestrained delight. They laughed and laughed till the leaves fell from the humble bushes; they stamped their feet and clapped their hands till the floor of the desert seemed to shake, and sparks from the fire went whirling away into the night.

Then, suddenly and unexpectedly, in the middle of his dance, the bush boy sneezed. He sneezed again and again and again (as he'd never sneezed before). Abruptly the pantomiming came to an end.

The sneezing had a curious effect on the bush boy. He seemed to grow suddenly weak. He passed a hand over his forehead, and his fingers came away damp. When he saw this dampness a great fear came over him. He remembered an old man he had seen in the tribal caves: an old man who had sneezed at the time of the rains, whose forehead had become damp with fever, whose body had been very light when, forty-eight hours later, they had lifted it onto its burial platform. He began to tremble. Slowly, uncertainly, he walked across to the fire. He lay beside it, close to its warmth; but he couldn't stop shivering.

The white children looked at the bush boy in astonishment. But neither went to him: the boy because in the last few days he'd witnessed so many incomprehensible changes of mood that he had come to disregard them; the girl for reasons of her own. Soon both brother and sister slept. But the bush boy didn't sleep. Not for many hours. He lay close to the warmth of the fire, but he couldn't stop trembling. And quite frequently he sneezed.

CHAPTER THIRTEEN

It was obvious, next morning, that the bush boy had caught Peter's cold. His nose was running, his eyes were heavy and his muscles ached. Long after sunrise he was still sitting beside the dying fire, too lethargic apparently to think of breakfast. Peter and Mary tidied up the camp, replenished the fire, cooked the last of the *yarrawa* and offered the bush boy a share—but he wouldn't eat. Then they waited: waited for him to move.

But he just went on sitting, hour after hour.

The little boy was worried. "I think he's sick, Mary."

"He looks O.K. to me."

"I'll ask him."

Peter went up to the bush boy.

"Hey, there! Are you O.K.?" He eyed him anxiously. " 'Cause if you are, we'd better be heading for Adelaide."

The bush boy blinked; came suddenly out of his trance. He saw the lubra and the little one looking at him anxiously and remembered that the valley-of-waters-under-the-earth was still five sleeps away. He got to his feet, slowly, and without a word struck south, through the scrub.

All that morning they walked in silence.

A little after noon the bush boy started to cast around, as if unsure of the trail. Twenty-four hours ago he'd have explained to Peter what he was looking for, but he was too preoccupied now. He soon found what he wanted: the claw marks of a food-searching bird. He followed the marks up, picking out a trail that the white children never even saw, a trail of toe-scratchings, odd feathers and droppings, a trail that led at last to a circular hillock, three feet high, a hillock built by the talegulla (bush turkey) out of earth and decomposing leaves. Inside the hillock, the bush boy knew, would be eggs, the eggs of the bush turkey, the fowl that knows no broodiness, that lays its eggs and wanders off, leaving the warmth of the decomposing leaves to hatch its deserted offspring.

There were fourteen eggs in the mound, each partitioned off from its neighbors by walls of decaying leaves. One by one the bush boy unearthed them: steaming, pink-tinted and the size of golf balls. The children roasted and ate them. The firm, nut-flavored flesh was nourishing; it satisfied their hunger, but sharpened their thirst. Of water there was no sign.

The midday rest was longer than usual, and once again the white children had to coerce the bush boy into making a start. His cold was coming out now; his nose was streaming, his eyes were heavy and his sneezes were interspersed by the occasional cough. When at last he did start off, his pace was slow, as if every step was an effort.

Peter tried to cheer him up, but without success. The Aboriginal had gone into a semi-trance; he moved like a sleepwalker, lost in a world of his own.

"Look, Mary!" The little boy was worried. "He isn't well. Can't you do something?"

"He's only got a cold, Pete. Like you had. Nothing to bother about."

"But look at his eyes. They look funny. What's he staring at?"

But the girl wouldn't look at the bush boy's eyes.

"He's all right," she said. "Don't fuss."

They walked all afternoon, all evening and a little way into the night, and when they did at last come to a well, its water was brackish and faintly salty.

The bush boy wasn't going to bother over a fire, but Peter and Mary, tired as they were, collected wood and persuaded the Aboriginal to help them get it alight. Then the three of them, utterly exhausted, lay down to sleep. Peter dropped off at once; Mary after a little while; but the bush boy stayed awake, hour after hour. He felt hot one minute and cold the next. Convinced that he was getting the fever-that-comes-with-the-rains, he kept feeling his forehead. And a little after midnight his fingers came away damp. He started to tremble then. He hoped the lubra and the little one knew how to make a burial platform: high off the ground, so that the evil spirits couldn't creep out and molest his body.

Next day the sun had risen before the children were on the move. They had no breakfast, and the bush boy was noticeably weaker. But at last they started off, heading south by west across the level plain. In the distance, heat-hazed and very far away, they could see a low range of hills. The bush boy pointed to the hills.

"*Arkooloola*," he said.

And that was the only word he spoke until their midday rest.

But a little before noon he came—if only for a moment—out of his lethargy.

It was Peter who saw the echidna first: a pair of

porcupine-like creatures scurrying between two clumps of yacca. He grabbed the bush boy's hand.

"Look! Food! *Yeemara!*"

The bush boy came suddenly to life. He snapped off a branch of yacca and leaped after the echidna. They heard him coming; they tried to escape in the only manner they knew, by diving under the ground, by burrowing into the earth as if it were chocolate marshmallow. But the bush boy was too quick for them. With a thrust of the yacca he blocked their getaway; with the end of the branch he prized them up to the surface. He unrolled them, skillfully avoiding their quills, and set them down on the sand. In the pouch of the female he found a tiny replica of herself: a frightened, blinking pup, whose quills were soft as chickens' down. Gently he put the mother down; set her free to tend her young; to raise the pup to a size more suitable for food. But for the male there was no reprieve. His deathblow was mercifully swift; his body was tossed to the lubra. They ate him, when the day was at its hottest, casseroled in eucalyptus leaves.

For a long time that afternoon the hills seemed to come no nearer; then, quite suddenly, the children were walking into their shadow.

They found an idyllic place to camp in the shade of an outcrop of rocks which ringed a diminutive water hole. They drank deeply, kindled their fire and settled down in the shade of a boxwood thicket for the night.

The bush boy's cold didn't appear to be any worse; indeed, if anything, he was sneezing and coughing less. Yet he seemed weaker, increasingly preoccupied, and the children noticed that his coordination was beginning to fail—twice, while making fire, the yacca rolled out from between his hands.

Peter was very solicitous. Seeing the bush boy huddled by the fire yet still trembling—he supposed with cold—he took off his shorts and tried to cover him up. And the Aboriginal seemed to be grateful. Peter looked at him thoughtfully, then at his sister. He had a sudden idea.

"Hey, Mary!" His cheerful shout echoed back from the rocks. "The bush boy's cold. Couldn't he have your dress?"

The girl's mouth fell open. For a second she stared at her brother in disbelief. Then she swung around and started to bank up the fire.

But the little boy wasn't put off.

"Why, Mary! Don't be mean. He's cold."

The girl said nothing.

Peter looked at her curiously. Her face had gone unexpectedly pale; her eyes, once again, were frightened.

"I think you're scared!" the little boy announced with unexpected relish. "Fraidy cat! Fraidy cat!"

Mary turned away. She hid her face in her hands. If only he wasn't so small; if only he was a few years older, then he'd understand.

She saw the bush boy looking at her, watching her. And she shivered.

The Southern Cross blazed out of a cobalt sky; the sundown wind faded to a whisper; and a pair of marsupial rats, their eyes aglow like luminous peas, hopped hesitantly around the camp. Mary threw a branch of yacca into the flames. The sparks crackled and flew; and the rats, with tiny ping-ponging hops, fled. The stars glowed like gems. The desert, like the children, slept.

Next morning Peter woke early. He yawned, stretched, looked first at the others—still asleep—then at the water hole. It looked cool and tempting: a rock-bound pool fed by a miniature waterfall cascading out of a hidden spring. He got up, strolled across, sat on the edge and dangled in an exploratory toe. The water was delightfully warm, and with a noisy belly flop, he dived in.

The pool was exactly the right depth: up to his armpits. Working his way to under the waterfall, he reveled in the cascading, sunlit spray. He stayed a long time in the water, soaking every pore of his sturdy young body. He noticed with satisfaction that his body wasn't white any longer; a week's continual exposure to the desert sun had tanned it a rich mahogany—only he hoped it wouldn't get any darker or he'd be black as the bush boy. At last, refreshed and invigorated, he wandered back to the campsite.

The bush boy was still asleep; but Mary had just waked up and he told her about his swim in the rock-bound pool.

The girl looked at the Aboriginal and saw that he was motionless, apparently fast asleep.

"You make up the fire, Pete," she said. "Can you do that? While I bathe?"

"Course I can do it."

She smiled, glad of his self-reliance, and made her way to the far side of the rock.

The pool was everything that Peter had promised. The girl took off her dress, ruefully noting its rents and tears, shook loose her hair and dived in. The water was crystal-clear and warm as a tepid bath. Lazily she swam across to the waterfall and let the spray cascade onto her naked body. She felt relaxed, washed clean of cares and doubts and fears. Sometime, she thought, some distant day or week or month, they'd come to Adelaide (or some other settlement); the bush boy she wouldn't think about; in the meantime the sun shone, there was water to drink, food to eat and Peter's cold was on the mend. She started to sing, gaily, swirling her hair from shoulder to shoulder.

Peter, meanwhile, had fanned the fire into a blazing pyre of yacca. And the bush boy had waked up.

He lay on his back, thinking. He wasn't used to thinking—most of his actions being dictated by custom and instinct rather than thought. But there was something he had to think about now, something vitally important: his burial table. Did the strangers know how to make it: high off the ground, so that the serpent that slept in the bowels of the earth couldn't creep out and molest his body? The strangers were such an ignorant pair; he couldn't leave anything to chance; he'd have to make sure they knew what had to be done.

He got to his feet, slowly, weakly.

If other things had been equal he'd have talked to the little one—he was on easier terms with him than with the lubra. But he saw that the little one was working: was collecting firewood, while the lubra, to judge from her singing and splashing, was merely washing her body. Tribal custom frowned on disturbing those who were working. And it never occurred to the bush boy to wait for a more propitious moment. He set off to find the lubra.

He climbed the outcrop of rock and saw her a little way below him, bathing in the pool. She'd taken off her strange decorations and loosened her hair so that it was no longer scraped up on the back of her head but flowed, long and golden, on the surface of the water. The bush boy had never seen such hair, sand-colored and trailing

like the comet that rides the midnight sky. He thought it
very beautiful. He lay down on the sunwarmed rock and
stared, admiringly.

Quite suddenly the girl looked up: looked up straight
into his eyes, into his staring, admiring eyes.

She backed away in terror. Her hands, sliding along
the bank, clutched at a loosened fragment of rock. She
pulled the rock free; grasped it firmly.

The bush boy came walking down to the pool. But at
the water's edge he stopped: stopped in amazement. For
the lubra was snarling at him; was snarling like a
cornered dingo, her nose wrinkled, her lips curled back,
her eyes filled with terror. He took a hesitant step
forward, saw the stone in the lubra's hand and stopped
again. Hatred was something alien to the bush boy, but
he couldn't fail to recognize the look in the lubra's eyes.
He knew, in that moment, that his body would never get
its burial platform.

He felt suddenly weaker, much weaker. Things were
happening that he didn't understand: didn't want to
understand. He looked at the lubra's frightened eyes and
snarling mouth and was appalled. The will to live
drained irrevocably away.

Slowly he turned. He walked a few paces back into the
desert; then he lay down in the shade of a mulga wood.*
The branches hung limply over him; the great puce-
colored flowers wept tears of blood.

---

* The mulga wood, to the Aboriginals, is the tree of sorrow, symbol
of the broken heart; for its appearance is sad and drooping, and its
flowers are perpetually wet with a crimson fluid, seeping out like
blood.

CHAPTER FOURTEEN

The yacca wood burned quickly, and Peter had a full-time job replenishing the fire. He couldn't think what was keeping the others; but he hoped they'd come soon—before he ran out of firewood.

At last he saw his sister scrambling down the outcrop of rock. Even from a distance he sensed that something was wrong; and when she came slowly up to the fire and held out her hands to the blaze, he noticed about her an unnatural calm, an air of too carefully imposed restraint. For a while neither spoke; then the girl picked up a branch and started to draw ash over the flames.

"Hey!" Peter was indignant. "You'll put it out."

She nodded. "We don't need it."

"Course we need it. How are we going to cook breakfast?"

"There's no breakfast."

She followed the point up.

"Listen, Peter," she moved closer to him. "There's no food here. So there's no point in staying. Let's move on."

He eyed her suspiciously.

"What's the rush? The bush boy'll find us food."

"Listen, Pete"—she was pleading now—"let's go by ourselves. Just you an' me. We'll manage."

His mouth started to droop.

"I don't want to leave the bush boy."

"He doesn't want to come, Pete. I know he doesn't."

He eyed her doubtfully, unconvinced. "How d'you know? You can't talk his language!"

She went on raking over the ash.

"I tell you," she said, "he doesn't want to come. I know."

A week ago he would have accepted her word; would have fallen in with her plans. But not now.

"I'm going to ask him myself." He strode off purposefully, heading for the outcrop of rock.

The girl made as if to run after him, to pull him back. Then she stopped; that, she realized, would do no good. She sat down by the dying fire. Her fingers plucked at the hem of her skirt.

After about ten minutes Peter came running back; out of breath.

"Mary!" His voice was frightened. "The bush boy's sick. He's lying under a bush. An' he won't move."

"Maybe he's asleep."

Peter looked at her in disgust.

"Course he's not asleep. He's sick. Come and look."

"No!"

The girl drew back.

"No!" she whispered. "I won't go near him."

They spent a miserable, frustrating day. Peter wouldn't leave the bush boy; Mary wouldn't go near him; and they had no food.

In the afternoon the little boy went wandering off up-valley. His sister followed.

"Where are you going, Pete?"

"To look for food."

She came with him eagerly, hoping this was the first step in their breaking away, in their going off on their own. But Peter wouldn't go far; after less than an hour he turned back, insisted on retracing their steps. They found no food.

Peter spent most of the evening carrying palmfuls of water up from the pool to where the bush boy lay motionless in the shade of the mulga wood. At first the Aboriginal wouldn't drink, but eventually he accepted a little—though Peter noticed he seemed to have difficulty in swallowing.

A couple of hours before sundown the white children went on another food hunt, this time down the valley. And this time, more by luck than judgment, they found a cluster of the yams-with-foliage-under-the-ground. They rooted up three apiece and carried them back to the camp. After a good deal of difficulty they rekindled the fire and covered the yams with ash. An hour later they were eating them, while the sunset wind rustled the boxwoods, and flying phalangers zoomed playfully from tree to tree.

Peter took one of the yams to the bush boy, but he wouldn't eat.

He seemed to be much weaker; to have lost all interest in what was happening around him. Yet his cold was certainly no worse, and all trace of fever had vanished. He simply lay there, his dark eyes becoming slowly more clouded, his body temperature gradually falling and his pulse growing imperceptibly weaker. Resigned to what he thought was inevitable, he was willing himself to death.

For a long while that evening Peter sat beside him,

holding his hand. There had always been a bond between the two boys—a mutual liking and understanding—and it was because of this that Peter now realized the bush boy was dying. He held his hand more tightly. After a while he noticed the bush boy's lips were moving. He bent closer.

"Arkooloola!" The whisper was unmistakable.

Peter ran to the pool, cupped his hands and brought back water. But the bush boy pushed it aside; he shook his head; with an effort he raised himself up.

"Arkooloola." He pointed at Peter.

"Me?" The little boy was astonished. "I don't want a drink."

"Arkooloola," the bush boy insisted. *"Yeemara."* He pointed first at Peter then at the hills.

It was some time before the white boy understood; only when the Aboriginal scooped together a ridge in the sand to represent the hills and traced a trail from one side to the other, did he get the gist of the message. Then he nodded, gratefully.

"I get it. Over the hills there's food an' water, *Arkooloola* an' *yeemara.* That's fine. Now you lie down."

The bush boy's eyes clouded over. He rolled on to his side, drew up his knees and lay very still.

Peter took his hand; squeezed it reassuringly. Then, struck by a sudden thought, he got up and walked across to his sister.

She was sitting beside the fire—about 200 yards from the mulga wood—drawing patterns in the sand with a pointed branch. She looked up as Peter approached.

"How is he?"

Peter was very matter-of-fact.

"I reckon he'll soon be dead."

"Oh, no! No. No. No."

She started to sway backward and forward, her hands over her face.

Her brother eyed her critically. Then he remembered what he'd come to ask.

"Do you think he'll go to Heaven?"

"I don't believe you." The girl's voice was muffled. "He's only got a cold."

"I'm afraid he won't. 'Cause he's a heathen, isn't he. He's never been baptized."

The girl got slowly to her feet. She started to pace up and down, torn by conflicting emotions to the edge of distraction.

"Are you sure he's really sick, Pete?"

"Course I'm sure. Come an' see."

For a long time the girl was silent. Then she said slowly: "All right, I'll come."

They walked across to the mulga wood, to where the bush boy lay in a pool of shadow. Beside him, the girl dropped hesitantly to her knees. She looked into his face, closely, and saw that what her brother had told her was true.

She sat down, stunned. Then very gently she eased the bush boy's head onto her lap; very softly she began to run her fingers over and across his forehad.

The bush boy's eyes flickered open. For a moment he was puzzled; then he smiled.

It was the smile that broke Mary's heart: that last forgiving smile. Before, she had seen only as through a glass darkly, but now she saw face-to-face. And in that moment of truth all her fears and inhibitions were sponged away, and she saw that the world which she had thought was split in two was one.

He died in the false dawn, peacefully and without

struggle, in the hour when the desert is especially still and the light especially clear.

The girl didn't know when he died. For she had fallen asleep. Her head had drooped, until her cheek rested on his, and her long golden hair lay tumbled about his face.

CHAPTER FIFTEEN

They buried him close to the water hole.

The little boy was surprisingly matter-of-fact and practical; he insisted on the Aboriginal being christened at the same time as he was buried—"otherwise he mightn't go to Heaven." Mary said nothing. She had a vague idea that it was too late for christening now; but that was something her brother need never know.

It was noon before they had finished—for the desert sand was hard to dig with boxwood branches and sharp-edged stones—and the children were tired and hungry. They had two yams left over from the night before, and these they ate, raw. Then they sat in the shade of the boxwoods and looked at one another.

It was Peter who took command. After a while he got to his feet.

"Come on, Mary," he said. *"Kurura!"*

"Where to?"

"Over the hills, of course."

The girl looked doubtful.

"Are you sure that's the way, Pete?"

"Course I'm sure. The bush boy told me. Over the hills there's food an' water."

"All right," she said. "Let's go."

They started to climb the valley. All afternoon they

kept in its shadow. And the ghost of the bush boy was with them in every passing plant and stone. For both children had fallen into his ways. They walked now with the bush boy's easy, distance-eating lope; their eyes—like his—were ever questing ahead, studying the terrain, picking out the most promising leads; and every now and then—as he had done—they plucked and ate the pea-sized water-containing pods that dangled from the straggling belts of bush violet—nature's thirst quenchers. It was the same that evening, when, an hour before sundown, they made camp. His ghost was in the yacca wood they picked for their fire, in the sun-warmed stones they chose for their hearth, in the roots of the wondilla grass and stalks of sugarcane they ate for supper. They lived as he had lived, like his shadows. Adaptable as adults could never be, they made the desert their home.

They hadn't mentioned the bush boy a great deal during the day, but now, with the flames a-flicker and the stars aglow, they missed him more, missed him with an added poignancy. Peter looked at the Southern Cross, aflame like the jeweled hilt of a sword.

"Mary," he whispered. "Is Heaven up there? Way up beyond the stars?"

"That's right, Peter."

"You reckon the bush boy's there?"

"I reckon he is."

She said it automatically, to comfort her brother. But in the same moment that she said it, suddenly and unexpectedly, she believed it. More than believed it. Knew it. Knew that Heaven, like Earth, was one.

When the children woke next morning they were

hungry—they had had no meat in the last thirty-six hours, nothing more solid than vegetables and nuts. Mary woke first. She stirred the fire, tossed on a fresh supply of yacca wood, then went wandering down to the water hole beside which they had camped. The shallow, mud-banked pool looked a likely place for fish, and the girl approached it hopefully. But a few yards short of the bank she stopped, listened. The sound of splashing was unmistakable: loud and playful. She crept forward and peered cautiously through the rushes.

In the center of the pool three of the strangest creatures were playfully gamboling over the water. The girl looked at them in amazement—they might have come from another world—then she ran noiselessly to fetch her brother.

Soon the two children were watching the platypuses at play.

There were three of them: mother, father, and half-grown child. The adults were about twenty inches long, four-footed, fur-covered and with enormous duck-like beaks. They were aquatic mammals—a link with the prehistoric past—web-footed egglayers, teatless milk producers—the lactic fluid being exuded through the female's skin pores, poison-fanged amphibians, with fangs in the hollow of the male's hind feet. No wonder the children stared in amazement!

Normally the platypuses were timid creatures, inordinately shy; but now, confident that they were unobserved, they dived, leapfrogged and darted about with gay agility. Then, quite suddenly, they vanished, for Peter, edging forward to improve his view, had trodden on and snapped a twig. It was a very small snap—the children never even heard it—but in a flash the platypuses dived, dived deep, went snaking through underwater entrances to their burrow beneath the bank. There, in the maze of their smooth, highly polished tunnels, they were safe.

The boy looked at his sister.

"Reckon they're good to eat?"

"Oh, Pete! I couldn't! Besides, we'd never catch them."

They agreed to forgo breakfast in favour of a swim.

Peter jumped feet first into the pool. After a while he started to mimic the platypuses. He pursed out his lips, quacked and bobbed and splashed, showering his sister with spray, driving her laughing onto the bank. His miming became more hilarious, more abandoned— shades of the bush boy and lyre bird—until at last the girl joined in. Together they squawked and splashed to exhaustion, then they lay on the bank, side by side in the drying warmth of the sun.

But they couldn't, Peter knew, stay by the pool forever. And soon they were on their way, following the course of the gently rising valley.

At first the valley was well shaded and softly colored, aglow with the gold of casuarinas, the creamy white of bamberas and the pink of gums and eucalyptus. But as the children climbed higher, the vegetation gradually became more stunted and the colors harsher, cruder. By midday they were traversing a rocky barren terrain, its only trees the drooping mulga woods, its only flowers the everlasting daisies: the flowers that never die, that live on, even after their petals, leaves, stalks and roots have withered away. It was lucky that Mary had had the foresight to gather a cache of bauble nuts, and these they ate, soon after midday, in the shade of a slab or rock.

The valley was ending now, petering out in a saucer-shaped cwm about two hundred feet above them. Mary studied the formation of the hills, shading her eyes against the glare of the sun.

"Are you sure this is the way, Pete?"

"Course I'm sure. The bush boy told me. Over the hills."

The girl said nothing. The hills, she knew, were higher than they looked. And they'd soon be leaving the shelter of the valley. She wished they had something in which to carry water.

They rested for a couple of hours, then pushed on.

The valley became barer, bleaker and progressively less inviting. Yet even here, in its upper reaches, it had a certain beauty, not its former beauty of woods and shades and gentle colors, but a bold, bizarre beauty—a kaleidoscope of strange pigments and exciting, unexpected contrasts. Soon the valley slopes fanned out, exposing new vistas, wider horizons, the whole range of the hills delineated sharply in the clear, hazeless air. Dead ahead there swelled up a smooth, symmetrical hummock, its slopes, flecked with mica, reflecting the sun like a massed array of heliographs. To the left rose a rugged mound of granite, smooth and scalloped as an Arizona mesa. While to the right towered a fantastic pyramid of wine-veined quartz: alternate layers of crimson, gray and black.

The children edged forward, dwarfed by the immensity of the hills.

A couple of hours before sundown they came to the cwm, and here, in the saucer-shaped depression between the slopes of mica and quartz, they made camp. It wasn't a very inviting campsite, being boggy and devoid of shade, but at least they were close to water, of a kind.

They had hoped to find, at the head of the valley, a cool, refreshing trickle filtering out of the rock. Instead they found themselves staring at a brackish, stagnant pool, its surface filmed by oil from decomposing leaves. For a long time the children regarded it with silent disgust. Then the ghost of the bush boy came to their aid.

"Pete!" The girl had a sudden thought. "Remember that pool we found in the salt pan. Remember how the bush boy sucked up water with a reed. Let's try that."

They searched for and found a couple of hollow reeds, reeds of the watermat grass. Mary remembered to plug one end with moss (as a filter); then they plunged the reeds deeply into the pool and sucked. And the water they drew up was clean and cool.

Their thirst was slaked. Their hunger remained.

It was Peter who, purely by luck, solved the food problem. He was idly stirring the pool with his watermat reed—and dragging all sorts of leaf mold and water plant to the surface—when he noticed a queer little shrimplike creature clambering out of the stirred-up water.

"Hey, Mary! There's food in the pool."

The girl came running, eagerly. But when she saw the "food" she wasn't impressed.

"He's too small, Pete. And all arms and legs."

"Maybe there're others."

Together they peered into the brackish water, but saw nothing.

"I know, Mary!" It was Peter's turn to think back now. "Remember how the bush boy killed the fish. Throwing stones. Couldn't we do that?"

"No good here. Stones would go squelch in the mud."

They stared disconsolately at the pool. Then the girl hit on the answer.

"I know. Let's stir up the mud. Anything in the pool will get choked. And have to climb out."

It worked like a charm, better than they had dared to hope. They collected a couple of branches, plunged them into the pool and churned up the mud. In seconds the water took on the consistency of soup, brown and heavy, creamed with mud and scum. And almost at once the yabbies—diminutive crayfish of the bush—came bobbing up to the surface. Choked and blinded, they fled their haunts at the bottom of the pool. Desperately, like drowning men, they struggled for the bank. Bedraggled, they hauled themselves up—out of the frying pan into the fire. For on the banks the children were waiting for them. They snatched them up, smashed their heads against the earth, killing them instantly. On and on the slaughter went, till a full three dozen yabbies (each between four and eight inches long) lay dead beside the pool.

It was Mary who called a halt.

"That's enough, Pete. Let's not kill any more."

The yabbies, roasted on fire-heated stones, made a delicious meal. The children ate their fill and still had enough left over for breakfast.

Soon, curled close together, they settled down for the night.

It was cooler in the hills, and they were glad of the warmth of the fire. The girl had dragged up an extra large supply of branches, and from these she picked out a couple of arm-thick trunks and tossed them onto the fire. The sparks flew skyward; wreaths of woodsmoke

drifted across the stars; down-valley a dingo howled at
the crescent moon. Charleston, and the circumscribed
life of its suburbs, was in another world.

They woke cold and coated with dew, but the resur-
rected fire warmed them quickly, and a breakfast of
yabbies put them in good heart. They collected another
two dozen of the miniature crayfish out of the pool—
for the way ahead looked barren and devoid of food—
then, Peter leading, they set off across the hills, skirting
the pyramid of wine-veined quartz.

The hills had a primeval grandeur. They had been old
when the Himalayas were first folded out of the level
plain. Their rocky slopes were hard, enduring
unchanging from aeon to aeon. The children traversed
them slowly: ants on a gargantuan tableau.

In the clear light, distances and angles were hard to
judge. Slopes that looked an easy ten minutes' stroll
turned out to be an hour's exhausting climb. And always
at the top of one rise was another—wave after wave of
swelling hillocks, always steepening, always climbing,
never dropping away, never falling into the longed-for
valley of which the bush boy had told them.

In silence the children plodded on, watched by blue
wrens and moffets that tucked their pin-thin legs beneath
them and scooted about the flattened rocks like mice on
inset wheels.

Soon the rocks became increasingly rugged and
broken, cut into lopsided rifts and faults, as though a
giant with an axe had used the hilltop as a random
chopping block. Among the faults strange colors glinted;
here the silvery fleck of nickel, there the dull, rusty gold
of iron. Unmined wealth, undiscovered, unexploited.

Then, quite suddenly, as the children rounded a shoulder of granite, they stopped, stopped dead in disbelief. For in front of them rose a whole hillside aglow with shimmering color: every shade of the spectrum sparkling, flickering and interchanging, a kaleidoscope of brilliance rioting in the midday sun.

Mary's eyes widened, her mouth fell open.

"Jewels, Peter! Jewels! Millions and millions of them."

But they weren't jewels. They were something even more beautiful.

As the children approached the hill they heard a low, high-pitched rustling, a soft vibrating hum that trembled the air. Then, to their amazement, the blaze of color began to move, shimmering, palpitating, rising and falling, as the butterflies opened and shut their wings. Suddenly, like bees, they swarmed—disturbed by the children's approach—and in a great rainbow-tinted cloud went swirling south toward the Victorian plains.

The hill lost its magic. The sun streamed down. The children plodded on.

At midday they rested for a couple of hours in the shade of a steep-sided ravine. Here they ate the last of the yabbies. To both of them, the shrimplike creatures tasted vaguely salty. And they had no water. The girl dozed, drugged to immobility by the heat of the sun, but the boy was restless. Soon he got to his feet.

"Come on, Mary," he urged. *"Kurura.* Maybe that valley's over the next hill."

But it wasn't. Nor over the next. Nor the next. Nor even the one after that, which they reached in the gold of a dying sun.

They camped for the night beneath a low shelf of

granite. They were hungry and thirsty now; exhausted and disillusioned. There was no wood for a fire, no water for a drink. The sunset wind was cold, and so, when they came out, were the stars: cold and uncaring, cold, uncaring and very far away.

Before they slept the children talked awhile in whispers.

"Pete!" The girl's voice was anxious. "You think we ought to head back tomorrow? Back for the water hole?"

"Course not!" The little boy was scornful. "The bush boy said there's water over the hills. We'll go on."

CHAPTER SIXTEEN

Dawn brought wreaths of mist, as the heat of the sun warmed the dew-wet rocks, making them steam like asphalt after summer rain. The children woke damp and cold, hungry and thirsty, their mouths dry and their voices hoarse.

"Come on, Mary." Peter's croak was harsh as a kookaburra's. "I don't like this place. Let's move on."

He led off, round a shoulder of smooth-grained granite. Both children moved a deal more slowly than the day before. Every step required a conscious effort.

They found that the shoulder joined onto a solid massif, a great wedgelike block of hills flanked by a subsidiary ridge which ran directly across their line of advance. On top of this ridge little puffs of cloud, sun-tinted fawn and pink, were rising and falling to the breath of unseen air drafts. Mary looked at the clouds, thoughtfully, hopefully. She tried to remember her geography lessons—in hot climates weren't clouds supposed to form over water? Maybe beyond the ridge they'd come at last to the longed-for valley. She said nothing to Peter—for disillusion, if it came, would be too cruel—but somehow her eagerness communicated itself to the boy; he quickened his stride.

But the ridge proved unexpectedly steep, especially its last hundred feet. Here the rock was smooth, devoid of vegetation, swept clean by wind, scorched bare by sun.

Toeholds and footholds were hard to find.

"Careful, Pete." Mary paused, wiped the sweat out of her eyes and pointed to the left. "Over there. It's not so steep."

Slowly, painfully, they inched their way higher.

The clouds had changed color now, changed from pink and fawn to a dazzling white. Like puffs of cotton wool in a sky of powder-blue, they bobbed and curtsied along the farther slope of the ridge, almost within the children's grasp. And below them Mary could see more cloud, stratocumulus, layer upon layer. Her hopes rose.

"Careful near the top, Pete. In case the other side's a cliff."

They reached the crest together—the longed-for crest, swept by a cool and moisture-laden wind—and stood, hand in hand, looking down on the valley-of-waters-under-the-earth.

They couldn't see much detail in the valley itself, for it was blanketed in cloud, but the general layout was clear. It was a rift valley, steep-sided, about three miles wide, splitting the hills like an axe cut. Through occasional breaks in the cloud the children could see belts of scrub and the distant gleam of water.

Peter danced on the crest of the ridge.

"Just like he told us, Mary. Food and water. *Yeemara* and *arkooloola.*"

The girl nodded.

For a moment the clouds drifted away, revealing a skein of billabongs, reed-lined, dotted with waterfowl, and beautiful as the river that ran out of Eden. Then the layers of stratocumulus closed up. But the children had seen their vision, knew they'd been led to the promised land. Hand in hand they scrambled and slithered into the valley-of-waters-under-the-earth.

CHAPTER SEVENTEEN

The girl lay on her side, propped up on one elbow, cutting the twenty-fourth notch into a branch of yacca. The boy watched her.

"How long have we been here, Mary?"

She counted the notches, first those on one side, then those on the other.

"Eight days in the desert. Sixteen in the valley."

It seemed to both of them much longer. The past, especially to the boy, was like another world.

They lay beside a shallow lagoon, both of them naked—for on their third day in the valley the girl's dress had been torn beyond repair by the claws of a koala. In front of them the reed-fringed water, motionless as glass, went looping away down-valley; behind them the hills towered up, their summits wreathed in cloud; on either side of them virgin forest, dark as a cathedral vault, sprawled almost to the water's edge. It was midday, and the valley-of-waters-under-the-earth lay motionless, asleep in the heat of the sun.

For a fortnight the children had wandered slowly up-valley, exploring the curving lagoons, the reedy marshlands and the belts of semi-tropical forest. They had found a number of animals, fish and reptiles, and a great multitude of birds; but of human beings there was never a sign. They had plenty to drink and plenty to eat—not always what they'd have chosen (for the water duck eluded their every trap and snare)—but at least something, fruit or vegetable, reptile or fish. Now they had come to an especially beautiful reach of the valley, and the girl, much to her brother's disgust, was preparing to make a home—"just a hut of reeds," she had said, "in case we want to come back." Peter had jibed at the idea of homemaking. "What do we want a house for?" he had asked. "If it rains, we can shelter in the forest." But the girl had seemed so disappointed, that he had agreed in the end to call a halt until the reed-home was made.

He wasn't, in one way, sorry to have an excuse to rest, to lie back in the short, sun-hot grass and assimilate all that had happened in the last few days. They had seen such wonderful things, especially since they had come to the valley . . .

They had gone first to the lagoons, to the chain of looping billabongs, fed by underground springs, which lay like a string of sapphires spilled into the hollow of the valley. At first they'd had eyes for nothing but the water: the clear-blue, longed-for water, which in a few wonderful moments took the harshness out of their voices, the ache from their throats and the fear from their hearts.

Then they had noticed the birds.

They were everywhere, in water and reeds, trees and sky; and they were quite fearless. The children stared at them, wandered among them, watched and observed them with a wonderment that increased with every hour of every day.

They saw the wood ducks, the ducks that nest in trees, that carry their young to water by the scruff of their necks, as a cat carries her kittens. They saw the tailless swamp coots, nibbling wild celery as they floated by on self-made rafts. They saw the snakebirds, with their long rubbery necks and pointed-dagger bills. And the jacanas—the legendary Jesus birds—walking the water on their long, disproportionate toes (that use the fragile underwater lily leaves as stepping-stones). They saw dabchicks and zebra ducks, marsh bitterns and pelicans. And late one evening they saw the dance of the brolgas.

They were looking for a place to camp when Peter saw them: a cluster of eight or nine long-billed, stalk-like birds, slim, silver-gray and elegant, standing one-legged at the water's edge. As the children watched them they saw no sign, but suddenly—as if at a clearly understood command—the brolgas came to life and moved gracefully into a circle. One bird took up position in the center. He was the leader, the leader of the ritual dance. Opening wide his wings, he began a stately pirouette, a slow-motion quadrille. The others followed his lead; in stylized step they pranced solemnly around the circle, their feet moving in perfect time, their wings rising and falling to the beat of unheard music. The dance went on for several minutes—more than five, less than ten—then, quite suddenly, it ended. As if at another command the brolgas broke circle, moved into a random cluster and took up their original one-legged stance gazing peacefully across the lagoon. The children passed within six yards of them, but they never turned their heads.

And the birds of the forest were as strange and wonderful as the birds of the lagoons.

The children never tired of watching them. They saw the mistletoe birds planting their crops, plastering tree trunks with the seeds of the parasites which would later provide them with food. They saw the hawks fanning their nests, bringing their eggs to the requisite temperature for hatching; the butcher-birds stocking their larders, impaling live beetles, moths and fledgelings on the thorns of the ironbark; and the riflebirds, gilding their basin-like nests with the cast-off skins of snakes.

At sunrise and sunset the bird songs were near-deafening, a diurnal cacophony of notes clear and limpid, bizarre and unmelodious—the soft cadences of pilot birds, the wolf-wail of soldiers; the croon of yellow-bellies and the sandpapery scour of the scissor-grinders. While at night even stranger sounds echoed among the moon-white trees. The cowlike moo of the bittern, the yap of the barking owl, the coo-ee of the brain-fever bird, and rising above them all, the nightmarish scream of the channelbill—a maniacal shriek which terrified the water rodents into scurrying flight, making them betray their presence to the hovering bird.

No less wonderful than the birds were the trees of the forest, with their parasitic flowers and vines.

The children had been a little afraid of the forest at first; it was so enormous, so dark and earthy-smelling, with tree trunks soaring skyward, and strange, evilly fashioned plants choking each other to death in a sludge of decomposing vegetation. To start with they had stayed on its edges, among maiden-blush of reddish brown and heartswood of emerald green. Then, becoming bolder, they ventured a little way in, to where sycamore vied with tulipwood, and the cassias dug their quinine-producing roots deep into the fertile soil. And at last they dared the center—the heart of the primeval wonderland.

Here they found a fantastic battleground of tree and creeper, parasite and vine; with the bodies of the vanquished decomposing in the humid soil. The trees soared skyward, slim and straight, seeking the life-giving sun. But around them, choking them to death, coiled the dodders—the predatory vines, sucking the nutriment out of their roots, gripping the trees with tentacles like tightening tourniquets. And intertwined with the dodders were the jikkas, headless, tailless, rootless, vegetable snakes, growing on and on, from either end, wrapping their vampire arms around anything they touched.

But, as the children were quick to see, even such a charnel house as the forest center was not devoid of beauty—the staghorns, their leaves rearing skyward like the antlers of mating deer, the rock lilies, their bells as white as virgin snow, and the orchids, dangling like gossamer clouds out of the primeval trees. They wandered through twisting tunnels, arcaded with vegetation through which the sun had never penetrated; they smelt the rich humid soil which had never felt the stir of a drying wind. At first they were filled with awe and amazement, but eventually, after three or four days of exploration, they became almost as much at home in the forest as they had been in the desert.

Together they watched the ant lion lying in wait for his prey, lurking at the base of his self-dug trap, waiting for a victim to come plunging in to his death. Together they watched the fisherman spider, lowering his single thread baited with sweet-scented adhesive saliva; then, when the bait was taken, hauling the thread in, hand over hand.

They saw the stick-like praying mantis, the blue-skinned, red-capped cassowary and—on their third day in the valley—they saw the koala.

They were on the fringe of the forest, collecting hips from the bush roses which grew in banks among the eucalyptus trees, when Mary half-saw, half-heard a movement.

"Look!"

She pointed to one of the trees. Halfway down its smooth-grained trunk was a moving ball of silver-gray, a koala, shifting from tree to tree, from one supply of gum leaves to the next. Quietly the children crept to the foot of the eucalyptus. Slowly, steadily, one leg at a time, the koala descended.

It was a mother koala, and clinging to its back was a cub, a harmless, fist-sized teddy bear: fat, tufted-eared, button-eyed and covered in smooth sleek fur.

When the bears were about three feet from the ground, Peter darted suddenly around the trunk. He grabbed the cub by the scruff of its neck, jerked it off its mother's back and thrust it into Mary's arms.

"Bet you never had a doll as nice as that!"

The mother bear was far too slow-witted to defend her offspring. But she didn't run away. She hung onto the eucalyptus, blinking her eyes in surprise. Then she started to moan—a low, pathetic, sobbing moan.

Mary's heart went out to her.

"Peter! She wants her baby back."

She tried to disentangle the cub, but its tiny claws were hooked tightly to her dress. The thin material, already rent and worn, gave way. There was a long ripping tear. The dress slid to her feet. The koala sobbed and moaned.

A week ago nothing more calamitous could have happened to the girl. But now, after her initial shock, she felt strangely unembarrassed, more concerned, indeed, with the cub than with her nakedness. Kicking the remnants of her dress aside, she bent down and very gently returned the baby to its mother's back. Instantly the sobbing ceased. The mother koala looked around, blinked her eyes, licked her cub, climbed down the last three feet of trunk and waddled off to another eucalyptus.

"Poor thing!" Mary said. "You should have known better, Pete."

When, after a fashion, the reed hut had been completed, the children moved on. Mary would have been happy to stay, but Peter was eager to explore the rest of the valley.

It was a week later that they came to the end of the valley, a sheer precipice of granite, at its base a dark cleft from which an underground spring seeped out in a continuous trickle. About a mile from the end of the valley the billabongs broadened out, forming a shallow reed-fringed lake, about three quarters of a mile across.

Here the children made camp beside the water's edge. They camped early, close to a patch of pink-tinted pipe clay, agreeing to explore the precipice the following morning. Well before sundown they were eating rose hips and bauble nuts beside a blazing fire.

Then Peter discovered the clay. Discovered that, when moistened, it could be used for drawing, for drawing faces on the smooth lakeside rocks. He called Mary, and together brother and sister experimented with pieces of moistened clay. They found that it drew like chalk on a blackboard; and soon the lakeside rocks were covered with drawings, crude but evocative drawings, drawings that would have been a psychologist's delight.

After a few experimental dabs and smudges, the children settled down to their respective works of art. Peter drew koalas, lizards and Jesus birds—symbols of their new life. But Mary drew girls' faces framed with glamorous hairstyles, dress designs that might have come out of *Vogue* and strings of jewels exotic as the Fifth Avenue advertisements—symbols of the life that was past. And after a while she drew something else, something even more revealing: a house. A simple outline: one door, one window, one chimney, one pathway lined with flowers—symbol of subconscious hopes and nightly dreams.

The sun dipped under the rim of the hills. The children left their drawings and stretched out, side by side, in front of the fire. Darkness, like a flood tide, crept quietly into the valley.

"Coo-ee, coo-ee!" sang the brain-fever bird. Over and over again. Down by the lake a bittern mooed among the reeds. A crescent moon lifted clear of the hills. The valley slept.

Next morning they smoothed out the ash of their fire. They were just setting off to explore the head of the valley when they saw the smoke. A thin spiral of woodsmoke, penciling the skyline above the opposite shore of the lake.

CHAPTER EIGHTEEN

The smoke rose lazily: a slender, blue-gray column, pencil straight. For a long time the children looked at it in silence.

Suddenly the column broke, changed to a succession of puffs, in sequences of three; one large, one medium, one small.

"They're signaling, Pete."

"Yes."

The boy looked first at the smoke then at his sister; he saw that her eyes were shining, her lips parted. In the ashes he traced a pattern with the toe of his foot.

"You reckon we ought to answer?"

She nodded, silently, with eyes for nothing but the smoke.

They raked over the ash, pushed in kindling wood and soon there rose from beside the bed of pipe clay an answering column of bluish gray, a misty spear saluting the morning sky.

"Bring a branch, Mary. A big one, with lots of leaves."

The girl knew what was wanted, something light enough to lift, but bulky enough to block off the smoke. Soon their column too was broken into a sequence of irregular puffs.

While the boy signaled, the girl watched the farther shore of the lake. Suddenly she saw movement. She strained her eyes, but the figures she had momentarily caught sight of merged chameleon-like into the background of reeds. For a while everything was very still. Then the figures appeared again; three ill-defined pin-points leaving their column of wood smoke and coming down to the lagoon. The sunlight glinted on three fountains of spray as the strangers dived into the lake. A second later three arrowheads of white were moving slowly toward them over the sunlit water.

"They're coming, Pete."

The boy left the fire. He came and stood by his sister. He saw she was trembling and took her hand.

"Don't worry, Mary. I'll look after you."

She squeezed his hand, gratefully.

"Do you think they're white men, Pete? Or black, like the bush boy?"

The children strained their eyes as the swimmers came steadily nearer. They swam in single file; and it seemed to Pete that their heads were black and abnormally large.

"I think they're black men, Mary. Black men with big heads!"

The girl nodded; she had come to the same conclusion herself. She had expected to be terrified at the thought of herself being naked and the strangers being black, yet now that the fact of their blackness had to be faced up to, she realized—unexpectedly—that she wasn't nearly as frightened as if they'd been white! Holding Peter's hand, she stood at the edge of the water, waiting.

The swimmers came splashing into the shallows. And now that they were nearer, the children could solve the mystery of the size of their heads: they were carrying bundles.

The first swimmer was a full-grown male, and perched athwart his shoulders was a child, a baby three-year-old, his fingers clutching his father's hair.

The second swimmer was an adult female, a smiling broad-faced gin. Her bundle was a young *warrigal,* a half-grown dingo pup, its body draped round the back of her neck.

The third and last swimmer was a lubra, about Mary's age, and strapped to the top of her head was a yam-laden dilly bag.

The man grounded his feet. He waded out of the water and set the baby down. He was a tall man, slim and sinuous. His hair was straight and jet black, his chest was cicatrized with a V-shaped, shoulder-to-shoulder weal, and he was quite naked. The women followed him, the water glistening on their skin like black pearls. The gin was well-formed, almost buxom; the girl, like Mary, slim and lithe.

The man's eyes were curious. He addressed himself to Peter.

"Worum gala?"

His voice was deep, yet strangely soft and lilting; like the bush boy's, only several octaves lower.

While Peter floundered into conversation, the women turned their attention to Mary.

Deeds speak louder than words, and the young black girl and the white quickly came to an understanding. The lubra opened up her dilly bag, and offered Mary a yam. The gift was accepted, and a handful of bauble nuts offered in return. The gin nodded and smiled, and a few moments later understanding turned to something deeper, when the baby, realizing he had missed a share-out of food, started to cry, and Mary picked him up. He stopped instantly and started to play with her hair, with the long golden hair that hung almost down to her waist.

And as the baby boy cemented friendship between white girl and black, so the *warrigal*—the dingo pup—served as a link between man and boy. For Peter loved dogs. The *warrigal* reminded him of his basenji way back in Charleston. He listened to the Aborigine with only half his attention; his eyes were on the dog. Suddenly, unexpectedly, he went scampering off—the sight of the *warrigal* worrying a sycamore branch was too great a temptation. In a moment boy and dog were joined in playful combat, splashing together in clouds of spray through the shallows of the lagoon.

For a moment the Aborigine blinked in surprise. Then he laughed. He saw that the womenfolk were happily sharing food, and lay down among the rocks.

After a while he saw the children's drawings.

He glanced at them casually at first, noting the crude inaccuracies of Peter's koalas and lizards, then his eyes passed to the girl's pictures. He sat up then, intrigued. He squinted at the hairstyles, seeking in them some clue as to the strangers' race or tribe. He got up and walked slowly down the line of drawings, peering closely at each. And at last, at the very end, he came to the house, to Mary's dream house—one door, one window, one chimney, one pathway lined with flowers.

"*Awhee! Awhee!*"

He sucked in his lips.

The gin came across, quickly, and together they peered at the dream house. After a while Mary, still carrying the baby, joined them. They looked first at her, then at the house.

"Awhee! Awhee!"

The gin's voice was filled with curiosity, almost with awe. She spoke quickly, excitedly, pointing first to the dream house then to the hills on the far side of the valley. And quite suddenly Mary got the gist of what she was saying. Hope surged up in her. Over the hills was a house. Not just a hut such as natives lived in, but a house like the one she had drawn, a white man's house, a first stepping-stone on the long, long trail that would, one wonderful and longed-for day, lead them back to home.

"Where? Oh, where?"

Her eagerness was something the Aborigines could understand.

The black man's eyes were sympathetic. Gently he took the girl by the hand and led her down to the sand at the edge of the lagoon.

Peter, seeing them talking so earnestly, left the *warrigal* and came and stood by his sister.

He saw the black man point first to a valley looping aslant the hills like a tired snake. The black man mimed the climb of the valley: his feet rising, his knees sagging. At the top he indicated that the children should sleep. He lay down on the sand and snored. The gin giggled. Then, with the point of a yacca branch, he traced a line heading east, into the rising sun. After a while the line broke, and with a couple of curves the Aborigine indicated a hill. Then, beyond the hill, the line went on. Soon came another, lower hill, and here, the black man indicated, there was water; he drew a circle, pointed to the lagoon and lapped like a dog. He also indicated food, yams; he drew them beside the hill and champed his teeth. And here too he indicated sleep; again the lying down and again the snoring. The children nodded. Next day the line continued east, toward another, higher hill. And here, at the base of the hill, it stopped—at a house. The black man drew it—one door, one window, one chimney, one pathway lined with flowers.

The children looked at each other. The girl's eyes were bright as the stars of the Southern Cross.

"Oh, Pete!"

She burst suddenly into tears.

Peter looked at the *warrigal* and the reeds and the red gums and the glistening expanse of the lagoon. He looked at the hills, the tired old desiccated hills with their vivid pigmentations of ocher, red and gold. And it came to him in a moment of truth that the things he had seen and felt and learned in the last few weeks he would remember for the rest of his life. He walked slowly across to the fire and collected the last of their bauble nuts. He stood for a moment looking not at the others but up and down the sun-drenched valley; then he went across to the Aborigine and held out his hand.

"Good-bye!" he said very formally.

The black man grinned and he too held out his hand.

Peter turned to the girl.

"Come on, Mary," he said. *"Kurura."*

He led the way along the shore of the lake.